Accidentally Together

by

Jade Winters

Accidentally Together

by Jade Winters

Published by Wicked Winters Books

Copyright © 2016 Jade Winters

www.jade-winters.com

ISBN: 978-1-532-93791-0

Other titles by Jade Winters

Novels

143
A Walk Into Darkness
Everything To Lose
Caught By Love
Guilty Hearts
Say Something
Faking It
Second Thoughts
Secrets
In It Together
Love Interrupted
The Song, The Heart

Novellas

Talk Me Down From The Edge

Short Stories

The Makeover
The Love Letter
Love On The Cards
A Story Of You

Chapter One

'They laughed at me. Said I was a freak.' The young woman sat opposite Emma, her long golden curls framing her oval-shaped face.

Emma swallowed hard. The hurtful things people said never failed to amaze her.

'Who told you that, Louise?' Emma prompted.

'My …' Louise hesitated, eyeing Emma cautiously.

'It's okay. You can tell me. Whatever you say goes no further than these four walls.'

'My friends. They say I need fixing.'

'Do you think you need fixing?'

Louise's gaze fell to the floor, and her body curled into itself. In a harsh, low whisper, she said, 'I don't know. I don't know what I feel anymore.'

Bracing her elbows on her crossed knees, Emma leant forward. 'Shall I let you in on something?'

Louise's head shot up, her expression full of guileless optimism.

Emma couldn't suppress the lopsided smile teasing her lips. On rare occasions, she would share snippets of her life with her clients to put them at ease, especially when their struggles mirrored hers so painfully.

'Yes … please,' Louise said and straightened, her posture open to the information.

'I'm gay.'

Louise's mouth dropped open and her eyes widened. Emma saw a million questions buzzing through her head.

'As a teenager, I was like you. A war raged inside me. Half of me knew who I really was, but the other half fought viciously to stay in denial.'

Louise's eyes filled with unbidden tears, but unlike so many of their previous sessions, self-hatred didn't burn within them.

'How—' The rest of the sentence stuck in Louise's throat, but Emma was sure of the question.

'How did I figure it out?'

Louise gave her a quick, hard nod.

Progress, Emma thought and continued. 'Something beautiful … something wonderful happened.'

An image of full lips and sparkling grey eyes flashed in her mind. Emma let the memories flood her, and familiar warmth spread through her body.

'Something so profound that it irrevocably shaped the person I am today.'

Louise took a long inhalation. 'What happened?'

Lost in thought, Emma twisted a thin silver band on her right hand. Louise waited patiently for her to fill the silence.

'School was difficult, as you can imagine.'

Louise nodded.

'My last year was especially tough. I was just beginning to come to terms with my sexuality. Even though I hadn't fully come out, my classmates were more than happy to make me feel like I was different at every possible opportunity.

'One day, as I was walking across the school grounds trying to get to my next class, the usual treatment ensued. People called me names and threw bits of paper at me. A few boys offered to "turn" me …'

Emma stalled. Even after years of distance and her own affirmations, the memories still left phantom cuts on her skin.

'Go on,' Louise urged.

A smile spread across Emma's lips. 'Then, out of nowhere, the most popular girl in school walked up to me.'

The memory of the sun caressing Lauren's beautiful blonde hair, turning it into a halo around her gorgeous face, pervaded Emma's mind.

She remembered Lauren striding towards her, her eyes determined and serious, the uniform, which appeared drab and lifeless on everyone else, showcasing her curves and femininity. Everyone hushed around them as she stopped in front of Emma.

Emma braced herself for another cutting remark. Lauren had always been a mystery to her—wildly popular, but separate from the pack, like a goddess among mortals. And while Lauren had never bullied her, with a million eyes on them, Emma was sure it would only take a second for Lauren to crack and copy everyone else.

Lauren's hand rose, and Emma winced, expecting a slap or a pinch, but what Lauren did devastated her far more. She stroked Emma's cheek and brushed the loose strands of hair behind her ear.

Everything around her faded—the noisy chatter, the twittering birds, the horns blown by angry commuters on the nearby road—leaving only Lauren and her mesmerizing grey eyes.

'What did she do?' Louise asked, her voice as hushed as Emma's memories.

Emma cleared her throat, trying to stay present. Her heart fluttered as she said, 'She kissed me.'

The sensation of that first kiss, those sweet lips pressed against hers, the delicious tingle permeating her body, and the absolute rightness of Lauren thrumming in her soul—it all confirmed what she'd always known.

Emma's arms encircled Lauren, and Lauren leant into the kiss.

Nothing else mattered.

Not Emma's fear.

Not her hatred or self-loathing.

This beautiful girl was kissing her, and Emma's entire universe narrowed to the feel of Lauren's lips.

'She kissed you?' Louise's disbelief was clear.

Emma did not miss a beat. 'Yes, in front of everyone. I expected them to say something, but Lauren had shocked them into silence. Then the most amazing thing happened.'

Louise's gaze was intense. 'What?'

'I stopped fighting myself. I turned my shame into pride. Don't misunderstand. I was still very much a misfit and a weirdo, but I was the weirdo with the hot lipstick lesbian girlfriend.' Emma smirked, and Louise snorted a laugh.

'Things were easier,' Emma continued thoughtfully, 'and clearer for me after that.'

Louise sniffled and asked, 'What happened? I mean with that girl? Did you guys stay together?'

Hope bloomed in Louise's eyes, hope for her future through Emma's past.

The old sadness, an ache heavy with regret and loss, pulsed in her.

'Sorry, no.' The memory of Lauren's eyes, her bright smile, the sigh on her lips as they kissed, cascaded like a waterfall in her mind. 'She suddenly left school and moved away. I never saw her again.'

'Was she your first love?'

'Yes.' *My only love.*

Chapter Two

Emma approached Chez Fred Café. She was late. *Damn*, she hated being late, especially when it wasn't her fault. Instead of the hour she'd planned on spending with her mum catching up on family gossip, she'd be lucky to enjoy her company for forty minutes—if that. *Forty minutes in six months.* At one point in her life, that had been the exception. Nowadays, it was the norm.

Narrowly avoiding a collision with a couple exiting the restaurant, Emma held the door open and stood at the threshold on her tiptoes, surveying her surroundings. Waiters and waitresses wove between tables in the bustling café. Despite it barely being midday, the majority of the tables were occupied, and a hum of conversation complemented the soft classical music playing in the background. Spotting her mother's mop of frizzy blonde hair, Emma hurried to her, hoping the perspiration oozing from her pores wouldn't leave two ugly wet patches under her armpits.

Without a word, Alex, her mother's husband, glanced up at her from lowered brows, his fingers fiddling with a saltshaker. Emma avoided his gaze.

'I know I'm late, but we were originally meeting at one.' To hide her agitation, she glanced over at a child having a full-blown meltdown a few feet away on the floor.

If the kid thinks life's bad at her age, wait until she reaches adulthood.

'You do realise we've been waiting since eleven thirty.'

She snapped her head back around at Alex's accusatory tone. 'To be fair, you guys changed the time and didn't exactly give me much notice. I was with a client when you texted. I couldn't exactly reply while she was spilling her heart out.'

Alex sighed. 'It's irrelevant now.'

Ignoring him, Emma removed her jacket and dropped a kiss on her mother's cheek. She then acknowledged her stepsister, Hope, with a hug.

'It's so good to catch up, Mum. I've been looking forward to seeing you for ages,' Emma said as she sat down and reached for the menu. She'd only had a cup of tea and a biscuit for breakfast, and she had every intention of making up for it. 'Shall we order lunch? I'm famished.'

'We're not stopping for lunch. Not here anyway,' Alex said. 'My mate, Dave, got us a table at the Shard.'

'The Shard! No! Really?' she said with no attempt to hide her delight. 'I've—'

'Your mum and me are going—by ourselves,' Alex said, cutting her excitement short. 'Do you know how expensive that place is?'

What the actual … Talk about replacing the dangling carrot with a sledgehammer.

Emma scanned the menu. What was the point in getting upset? The Shard was only a sodding restaurant that served the yummiest food ever! Or so she'd gathered from reading the rave reviews on TripAdvisor. 'Oh, for a minute I thought—'

'Wait … we wanted to give you your birthday present first,' Stella said, reaching down beside her. She set a bag onto her knees and withdrew a nondescript, medium-sized box. Flipping the lid off, she plonked it down in front of Emma. 'There you go, sweetheart. Happy birthday.'

Emma gaped at the object inside the box while her mind scrambled for something to say. Her gaze flicked to her mum then to Alex then back to her mum.

Hoping she had achieved the correct facial expression, she said, 'Wow. What can I say? They're … great!'

'Are you sure you like them?' Stella asked, frowning.

'Are you kidding? What sane person living bang in the middle of London wouldn't be impressed with a pair of …' She glanced inside the box again. 'A pair of binoculars?'

'That's good, 'cause we weren't sure what to get you,' Stella said. 'I told Al how much you loved looking up at the sky when you were little …'

Emma thought it best not to mention that the actual likelihood of seeing anything in the night sky was practically zero due to light pollution.

'And since we couldn't afford a telescope,' Alex said, his deep voice drowning out Stella's, 'I suggested the next best thing. It was by chance I found them in the garage when I was having a clear out the other day.'

'You found my birthday present in your garage?'

Can this day get any worse? Surely not!

'Yep. Waste not, want not, as they say,' Alex said. He looked extremely pleased with himself.

Smug bastard. Emma shot a look at Hope, who was struggling to keep a straight face.

'Right, now that's over with, let's get a move on, Stell.' Alex pushed his chair back. 'I want to make the most of this afternoon.'

'What do you mean, "get a move on"?' Emma asked. 'Aren't you even going to have a coffee with me, Mum? They serve one killer cheesecake—your favourite. I can vouch for it being the most delicious one I've ever tasted. Do you wanna try some?'

'Best not, Stell,' Alex said and stood. 'It'll only spoil your lunch.'

Emma flicked back her long, dark hair. 'I'm sure one bite won't make much difference.'

'No, Alex is right. I best not,' Stella said and leant down to pick up her handbag from the floor.

'Fine, go then,' Emma said, throwing her hands in the air. 'It's not as if this is a special birthday or anything. Thirty's no biggie.'

Stella dropped her bag and gave Alex an imploring look. 'Do we have time for one coffee, Al? It is her birthday.'

'All right, just the one. But make it quick.' Alex's face darkened with annoyance as he reclaimed his chair. He caught the attention of a waiter by clicking his fingers and beckoned him over.

'Thirty. I can't believe you're that old already …

and still single.' Stella fussed with her hair as she said this, appearing nonchalant, but her words cut deep into Emma's self-esteem. It might have been slightly amusing had it not been true.

Chapter Three

The hustle and bustle of London was in full swing outside Braithwaite House in Vauxhall. Behind the entrance door, Lauren pressed her forehead against the glass, her eyes narrowed to slits as she observed every stranger passing by. Not for the first time, she regretted returning to London, but the opportunity had been too good to turn down, despite the risk. Sensing there was nothing to be alarmed about, Lauren pulled open the heavy door and stepped out under the canopied entrance. Turning towards her destination, she paused.

Come on, come on. You can do this. Just put one foot in front of the other and go. It was silly to feel apprehensive after so many years had passed, but being back in London for the first time since it had all happened unnerved her.

She started down the pavement and had barely walked a hundred yards, when, without warning, a hand closed over her right shoulder from behind. Panic overrode her mind. Her temples thumped and a faint buzzing filled her ears. Instinctively, she grabbed the wrist, twisted it with all her strength, and she spun around to face its owner, ready for a showdown.

A slim man around the same height as her, sporting a wayward mass of hair and dressed in a scruffy t-shirt and black jeans, stared back at her. He looked more like an immature man-child than the imposing monster she'd been expecting.

His thin face creased in pain, and he yanked his hand back. 'Jesus, Lauren, easy. You could've broken my wrist. It's me, Mike. Remember? From school?'

Lauren gawked at him, frozen. Her hammering heart slammed against her ribcage. No one had called her that name in public for years. Not since …

'You really don't recognise me, do you?' Honest confusion rose in his voice. 'I haven't changed that much, have I?'

Shit, and neither have I by the look of things. Lauren pulled her black hoodie over her head. She had deliberately dressed down in jeans and a leather jacket, naïvely believing she could blend in with the hundreds of other ash-blonde women in London. *Obviously not.*

'You're mistaken,' she snapped. 'My name isn't Lauren.'

Mike's eyes burnt a hole in her back as she scurried down the road.

Before she reached the edge of the pavement to hail a taxi, he called out,

'Who you trying to kid? I never forget a face. Especially yours, babe. Never!'

Lauren jumped into the back of the cab and gave the driver the address. Slumping against the hard leather seat, she willed herself to calm down and stop blowing innocent incidents out of proportion. *Okay, so he recognised me. Big deal. He didn't see what building I came out of—or did he? Great, paranoia strikes again.*

Gulping down the bile that had heaved up into her

throat, she twisted around in her seat to look at Mike, who was still standing in the middle of the pavement. She remembered him all right. How could she forget? He was one of the creepiest people she had ever met.

By the time the taxi dropped her outside the Cotes House Art Gallery, Lauren's apprehension had turned to excitement at the prospect of having her very first exhibition in London. Though she'd had several exhibitions throughout Europe, holding one on her home turf felt special.

She opened the door and caught sight of Frankie, her long-time agent, leaning against the wall, legs locked at the ankles. He was tall and powerfully built, with a thick, dark tangle of hair. A tight white t-shirt and red waistcoat covered his muscular torso and his thick thighs were encased in a pair of fitted jeans. In front of him, a thin woman, no older than twenty, hugged a folder to her chest as she rocked back and forth on her heels.

Before Lauren could announce her presence, the entrance door slipped from her grasp and closed with a bang. They turned in her direction.

'Vikki, darling, you made it,' he said, pushing off the wall and gliding towards her with open arms.

'Am I too early?' Lauren stepped into his embrace and gave him a tight squeeze.

'You, my darling, could never be too early.' Frankie drew back and, with one arm, gestured to several framed black-and-white photos adorning the walls. They were part of Lauren's 'Unseen Collection,' due to be exhibited at the gallery in two weeks.

'Well, what do you think? Impressive, huh?'

Lauren gave a slow nod. She gazed at the images as if seeing them for the first time. Still haunted by the despair in the eyes of some of her subjects, she moved away from Frankie to stand before the photographs of individuals going about their daily lives in Paris—strangers who had been caught in the lens of her camera, totally unaware of her presence. *The omniscient one*.

She knew that haunted look well. It was one she saw in her eyes often enough.

'How're you settling in the apartment?' Frankie asked, breaking the spell.

Lauren turned to him. 'Better than expected.'

'That's what I like to hear.'

'Renting through Airbnb is much better than staying in a hotel. It's exactly what I needed.'

'Good! But if for any reason you want a change of scenery, you can stay at my place, okay?'

Lauren shook her head. 'As soon as the show's over, I'm going back to Paris. No two ways about it.'

'Well the option's there. Right, let's grab some coffee and then we'll get down to business. Molly, sweetheart,' he called out to the woman he'd been speaking with. 'Two coffees, please. One with milk and two sugars.'

Molly nodded and disappeared through a set of doors at the back of the gallery.

Frankie pointed to a stack of frames leaning

against a wall. 'If we can sort out which ones you want where, that'll be half the battle. I have an art journalist lined up to interview you tomorrow, and—'

'They're aware of the rules, aren't they?'

'Of course, darling. They get the interview on the condition that they only print your work, no photos of you. It's all sorted, don't worry.'

'I try not to, but I can't be too careful.'

Frankie gave her a sympathetic look. 'I know.'

'I had a run-in with someone from school on the way here.'

'Really? Who?'

'This guy called Mike. He's the kind of person you always feel uncomfortable around, his eyes scan you like an x-ray machine.'

'Do you think he—'

Lauren wrapped her arms around herself. 'Who knows? It could be anyone.'

'You know you're safe with me, right?'

Before she could reply, the clicking of high heels on the tiled floor announced Molly's return. She came into view, heading towards them with a mug in each hand.

'Great. Here's the coffee,' Frankie said, clasping his hands together. 'Shall we begin?'

Lauren was grateful for the interruption. Frankie wouldn't have been impressed with her answer. The truth was she didn't trust anybody—not even him.

Chapter Four

Alex ordered three coffees without consulting anyone on their preferences. Emma stared at him blankly. She opened her mouth to ask where he got off treating them like children, but nothing came out. What was the point? The much awaited 'lunch date' had already been spoilt.

'So what've you got planned for tonight, birthday girl?' Hope asked.

Absolutely nothing! 'Oh, you know, the usual,' Emma murmured.

'What's that then?' Hope pressed, humour dancing in her eyes.

Unfortunately, Hope wasn't sitting close enough for Emma to kick her under the table for putting her on the spot, so she settled for throwing her a venomous glance.

'Actually, Kelly and the girls are taking me out for drinks after work for an all-nighter.'

'That'll be nice. I don't think I've met Kelly before,' Stella said. 'Is she one of your special friends?'

Hope hid her mouth behind her hand, but not before Emma glimpsed her row of white teeth.

'No, Mum, she's not my girlfriend. Just a work colleague.'

'If only you'd meet a nice young man, you could settle down and have children. I hate to think of you alone, especially at your age.' Stella's voice had turned arid.

'At my age? I'm not exactly a sixty-year-old spinster or a "failure". And there's no way on earth I'm going to settle down with a man just because I'm despera—I mean single.'

Making a show of examining the binoculars, she mentally ticked off what she had achieved in her life: *I own an apartment. I'm in a job I like—no, love. And?* Her mind blanked. *Come on, I must have more than two achievements.* If she did, her stubborn brain refused to reveal them. *Okay, I'll have to come back to that,* she told herself, convinced her memory just needed a jump start.

Right, now for the things I still want to do. I definitely want to travel more. Fiji, New Zealand. Maybe get a furry companion? She questioned this and decided she wanted to wait until she upgraded her living conditions by moving into a house with a garden. *I want to feel more than like I'm playing a role in life. I want to feel important to someone and be truly loved.* An involuntary tightness gripped the back of her throat. *I want to feel that excitement in my stomach, like I did fourteen years ago.*

Why did her mum always assume she was single by choice, as if it was her fault the women she met didn't live up to the fantasy in her head? She cursed herself daily for this affliction, but her heart simply refused to settle for second best.

Emma rested the binoculars on the table.

'Anyway, I'd be more worried about Hope,' she said in an attempt to divert her mother's attention away from her. 'She's thirty-one and still takes her dirty clothes to the laundry for a service wash.'

'Only because I have better things to do with my time,' Hope responded.

Emma's face twisted into a sneer. 'Like what, post selfies on Facebook?'

'Now, now you two, stop bickering,' Stella said.

Hope stuck her tongue out at Emma then said, 'We're not bickering. It's called banter. It's what adults do when they're too old to fight.'

A waitress approached the table. Smoky grey eyes briefly met Emma's, then without saying a word, she laid out three coffees on the table. Emma watched her swagger to the bar and whisper something to her colleague, who looked over at her. *They're probably taking the piss out of my binoculars.*

Alex picked up the receipt and scanned it. 'Bloody hell, have you seen this, Stell? Three quid for a measly cup of coffee.'

He took out his wallet and fished inside.

'Don't worry about it. I'll cover it,' Hope said.

'It's all right, I've got it,' he said. 'Thankfully birthdays are only once a year.'

Stella readily agreed. 'I'm glad I only had the one child. How people afford more, I'll never know.'

'All those bloody benefits and what not the government doles out like sweets, that's how,' Alex said.

Hope gritted her teeth. 'Please, Dad. Do we have to have this conversation again? We all know your views on immigration and single mothers.'

He cracked his knuckles, causing Emma to wince. 'It's the truth, isn't it?'

The conversation soon reached a stalemate. Stella broke the tense silence with chatter about her bridge club, while Alex kept a watchful eye on their cups.

When Stella took her last sip of coffee, Alex said, 'Let's get out of here before they charge us for breathing the air.'

He threw the exact money on the table to cover the bill.

'Good idea,' Emma said. She put the lid on the box, scooted her chair back, and got ready to leave.

Outside, standing in the middle of the pavement, Alex patted the pockets of his jacket and trousers. 'Where've I put my sodding keys?'

Emma drew in several long, deep breaths. Alex misplacing his car keys was such a regular occurrence that she had suggested he keep them on a chain around his neck. *Preferably a tight chain!*

'Calm down, Alex. Check inside your jacket,' Stella suggested.

Alex did as she had advised, and after a few seconds, his hand reappeared with his keys in it.

'Honestly, Alex, I don't know what you'd do without me.'

Alex pulled Stella into an embrace and kissed her on the mouth. 'Wither away and die, my lovely.'

Stella gave him a rueful laugh. 'Oh, you're such a charmer.'

'That's why you married me, isn't it?'

Emma glanced at her wristwatch. As much as she'd love to stand around and bear witness to their gushy display of affection, she'd prefer to be at work.

'Right, Mum, Alex, am I seeing you at Easter?'

Stella stepped forward, put her arm around Emma's shoulders, and pulled her close. 'We'll let you know if we haven't made plans.'

Emma stiffened and eased out of Stella's embrace. 'Yeah, well, let me know in advance, 'cause I might have plans myself. Have a great afternoon you two.'

'We will. I'll get Stell to email you some pictures,' Alex said as he opened the car door.

'Thanks,' Emma replied, only half listening. 'I look forward to it.'

Emma and Hope watched from the pavement as their parents' blue 4x4 Mercedes disappeared down the street.

'Thank God that's over,' Hope said.

'No comment.'

'I can't believe how insensitive your mum can be sometimes.'

It was nothing new. Why it still pissed Hope off, she didn't know. Emma had been relegated to the backseat when her mum and Alex married fifteen years earlier. Their once close mother-daughter relationship was no longer.

'It really doesn't matter.'

'Doesn't matter?' Hope planted her hands on her hips. 'It's your thirtieth birthday and she couldn't spare you an hour. Then to add insult to injury, they gave you some old toot my dad found in his garage, and you're saying it doesn't matter?'

Emma's brows drew together. 'It's the thought that counts, I suppose.'

'The thought?' Hope nudged her with her shoulder. 'Be honest. You're fuming inside, aren't you?'

Emma opened her hands in a gesture of defeat. 'Okay, okay, just a little—'

'A little?'

'All right, a lot then. It's not so much the gift. I can't believe my mum didn't want to spend time with me.'

'If you gave me a pound every time you said that—'

'Yeah, I know, you'd be a millionaire,' she finished for her.

'Exactly. So where're you going for drinks later?'

'Nowhere.' Emma could admit the truth now that her mum was gone. 'But thanks for needling me about it. Some great stepsister you are.'

'You shouldn't be pissed off with me. You should be calling out your mum on her behaviour. She treats you like a distant relative she's obliged to make time for.'

'Come on, she's not that bad. You're making her sound like—'

'The bitch she is?' Hope suggested.

'She's not a bitch. She's just wrapped up in your dad, that's all. I'm glad she has someone and isn't alone.' *Unlike me!*

A strand of dark hair fell onto Hope's forehead, and she brushed it away with the back of her hand. 'I must have been born inside the wrong body or something, 'cause I'll never understand women for as long as I live.'

'There's nothing to understand. It is what it is.'

'If you say so,' Hope said, looking wholly unconvinced.

Dark, heavy clouds amassed, blackening the sky. A droplet of rain fell on the tip of Emma's nose. Why did her birthday have to fall right in the middle of January, when the weather was absolute pants? It was either raining or … well, raining.

'On that note, I'd better get going.' Emma swung her bag over her shoulder and started down the road.

'So what're you really doing tonight?' Hope called after her.

'Flaking out in front of the telly with a bottle of wine.'

'Fancy some company?'

Emma turned around but continued walking backwards. 'Sure.'

'We can stargaze with your new binoculars.'

'Don't you mean cloud gaze?' she said, feigning an enthusiasm she was far from feeling. 'Can't wait.'

Chapter Five

The rain hammered the pavement as Lauren arrived at her apartment building. The day had been productive, and she was happy with the way the exhibition was shaping up. After a gruelling few hours of indecision, she had finally worked out the placement and order of the images.

Shaking out the umbrella Frankie had lent her, she bypassed the lift in the lobby and headed straight for the stairs.

Before ascending, she peeked between the gap in the stairwell, looking and listening for anyone coming down. Satisfied she was alone, she bounded up the carpeted stairs two at a time, slowing her pace at each landing to listen for anyone descending.

Upon reaching the twentieth floor, she used the wall to steady herself as she walked down the hallway, panting. The building was thirty stories tall, and she was relieved she hadn't rented the penthouse like she had initially intended.

As soon as she entered the apartment, she walked straight into the kitchen. Though it wasn't very large, it had all the mod cons a kitchen needed: microwave, double oven, and most importantly, a dishwasher. She grabbed a bottle of water from the integrated fridge and took several gulps between breaths, her lungs burning with the need for air.

Lauren discarded her jacket and strode into the homely L-shaped living room. Prints of Banksy artwork hung on the walls and fluffy pink cushions were piled on a large fabric sofa. Passing by a glass dining table with four leather high-back chairs, she slid open one of the huge double-glazed windows, parted her lips, and drew in a mouthful of cool air. She inhaled for three seconds and exhaled for five until her breathing levelled out, but she remained at the window, drinking in what she could of the London skyline. To the left, the MI6 building—a post-modern concrete and glass Aztec temple—stood tall and imposing. Its presence was strangely comforting. The thought of all those spies close by added a sense of safety. *My very own James Bond on call— if only.*

Straight ahead stood an apartment building identical to hers.

Movement in one of the rooms directly opposite caught her attention. Squinting, she could just make out a woman with long plaited hair. She was folding laundry and piling it in a stack with her back to the room. Lauren watched as a dark-haired man snuck up behind her, and the woman spun around, knocking the washing to the floor. The man brought forth a spray of flowers from behind his back, and the woman fell into his arms. Seconds later, they left the room, holding hands.

Lauren next saw them in the bedroom. The man walked over to the window, loosening his tie, and closed the blinds. The loving scene reminded Lauren of Fiona. Had they looked that happy and in love to onlookers?

She spat out the strands of blonde hair a clammy wind had blown across her face. *However we looked together doesn't matter now.* As of seven months ago, Lauren and her ex were through. Done, dusted, finito!

How did it happen? How could a woman declare her love for you, whilst seeing someone else behind your back? Fiona's excuse for cheating was that she needed to *find* herself. She needed time.

Time. That's exactly what Lauren had given her when she packed her bags and ended the relationship. Now all Lauren wanted was time for herself and lots of it. She should have known better than to think a relationship with someone as selfish as Fiona could have worked. But she'd been smitten with the tall, dark-haired, athletic woman, and she had ignored the red flags telling her things wouldn't work out. *Was I ever being realistic to think they would?*

Her phone buzzed, and Lauren groaned when the caller ID lit up. Knowing Fiona wouldn't give up if she didn't answer, she connected the call. Swishing her hair aside, she put the phone to her ear.

'Yes?' she answered, letting her irritation ring loud and clear.

'C'est moi.'

'I know.' *Unfortunately.*

Silence.

''Ave you been avoiding my calls?'

Lauren rubbed her temples with the tips of her fingers. She was certain Fiona had lost the plot. 'Avoid your calls? Why on earth would I do a thing like that?'

'So you're okay?'

'Yes, I'm fine. I've never been better.' *Especially since I threw your cheating arse out of my life.*

'Look, we need to talk.'

'No, I'm busy.'

'Unpacking?'

'Yeah, unpacking.' She glanced at the unopened suitcase by the sofa. Ready to go, just in case.

'Dibs is pining for you. 'e misses you.'

Lauren pictured Fiona's scruffy, wire-haired Jack Russell and the corners of her mouth turned up despite herself.

'I miss him too,' she mumbled.

'What about me?'

'What about you?'

'Do you miss me?'

'Fi, it's been seven months. You need to stop this. I wish you would accept it's over and move on with your life like I have,' she said in a monotonous, but firm voice. Fiona had hurt her in the worst possible way, and Lauren hated being hurt, by anyone.

'N'importe quoi!'

Lauren disconnected the call. Immediately, the phone rang again. Pressing the power button, she turned it off and threw it on the sofa.

Lauren wound a strand of hair around her finger. Fiona's call had put her on edge. Despite her efforts to convince herself everything was okay, she feared something was bound to blow up in her face and send her scuttling back into hiding. She'd told herself that things were different. She was back in the city, older, and under a pseudonym. Nobody knew who she was or where she was. Nothing could happen to her, could it?

Then why did she wake up in the middle of the night unable to breathe, with her heart pounding? Why did her eyes have dark shadows in them?

Because you can walk away from the past, but it still whispers your name in the dark, taunting you.

Chapter Six

During times like these, when darkness blanketed the city, Emma regretted living in a two-bedroom apartment. The spacious accommodation somehow reinforced her loneliness. As much as she'd tried to fill her home with multi-coloured tables and chairs from Ikea and oversized fabric sofas from DFS, the pressing silence was a constant reminder that she was alone. It was crazy when she thought about it. Over eight million people lived in London. How could she not find her soulmate? No one serious had been in her life since forever.

That's what happens when you fall in love with a fantasy. But what a fantasy. Long, lustrous hair. Dark, brooding grey eyes. A luscious mouth so full and soft, ripe for kissing. And—*Oh God, don't let me even think about her fit body.* A sensual, hot rush flooded downwards. *After all of these years, she still has an effect on me.*

Before Emma could dwell on the memory of Lauren any further, the doorbell chimed. Overwhelmed by the memory, she stood too quickly and banged her knee against the coffee table. Rubbing the sore spot, she limped to the door. Emma lifted the intercom phone then buzzed Hope in before leaving the front door ajar and returning to the living room.

'For you.' Hope handed her a gift bag in one hand and a bouquet of flowers in the other as she walked in a few minutes later.

'Sweet,' Emma said, forgetting about the dull ache in her knee. She peeked inside the bag. 'Ooh pink champagne and raspberry truffles. You know how to treat a girl, don't ya?'

Emma gave Hope a hug then led the way to the kitchen. She gestured for Hope to take a seat at the table while she filled a vase with water.

'How was work?' Hope asked.

'Let's just say I was glad to escape today. Tell me something?' she said, untwisting the wire from the champagne bottle. 'Why are women so bloody bitchy? I mean seriously, we're all at work trying to make a living, but there always has to be one queen bee making it shit for everyone else.'

'I take it Wendy's pissing you off?'

Emma snorted. 'When isn't she? Honestly, that woman's snooty attitude makes my blood boil. She's always looking down on people. She was actually complaining about the way the kids who come for counselling dress. Can you believe that? Like it really matters.'

'I must admit, after meeting her for the first time, I wondered why such a hard-nosed cow would be in a job that requires compassion and understanding.'

'That's neither here nor there when you're good at getting sponsors to part with their cash. In that sense, she's a star.'

'That's why I prefer working from home. The less contact I have with people, the more I can convince myself that humanity on a whole isn't devolving. You know the saying, "The more people I meet, the more I like my dog". Well, that's me, and I don't even have a dog!' Hope laughed sardonically.

Emma eased the cork from the bottle with only the slightest *pop*, poured the fizzy liquid into two tall glasses, and handed one to Hope. 'Some of us aren't lucky enough to work for ourselves.'

'Believe me, I count my blessings every day.' Hope lifted her glass in a toast. 'Happy birthday.'

'Thanks.' Emma raised her glass and took a sip of her champagne. The bubbles danced in her mouth, and she licked her lips. 'Hmm, now this is nice.'

'Do you wanna hit a bar and get hammered?'

Emma looked down at her jogging bottoms and slippers. 'I haven't got the energy to change again. I was gonna order pizza and watch a film on Sky Movies.'

'Or better still,' Hope said, scrambling to her feet. 'We can check out the sky with your birthday present. You never know, we might get lucky and spot a UFO.'

'Yeah right.'

'Come on, don't be a spoilsport. You might as well try them out.'

'Oh, all right. Let's finish this bottle first, then I'll go and grab them,' Emma said and took a swig of her drink.

An hour later, they were standing on Emma's small balcony, which she referred to as her garden in the sky. Wilted plants and flowers lined the railing, which she had every intention of reviving once spring arrived.

'Just as I thought,' Hope said. 'I can't see anything.

Not even a plane's visible in that miserable, dull sky.'

Emma looked up. 'Maybe it'll be better in the summer?'

'Like I'm waiting for the summer. You know what we can do?'

'What?' Emma was feeling tipsy and desperately wanted to go inside; a double cheese meat feast pizza beckoned.

'Some serious spying.'

'What, looking at people in their homes? No thanks. I'm no pervert.'

'Go on. It's only a bit of fun.'

'What if someone sees us?'

'We're twenty-two floors up. Who's gonna see us?'

Emma shrugged, mortified at the thought of spying on people. 'I dunno. I feel a bit uneasy about it, that's all.'

'Okay, goody two-shoes, you don't have to look if you don't want to.'

'Oh, all right then,' Emma said. 'But promise me that if anyone's naked or doing the deed we'll stop looking.'

'Boring, but if you insist. Now let's see what your neighbours get up to behind closed doors.' Hope lifted the lenses to her eyes and swivelled her head from left to right.

'Can you see anything?'

Hope's nose twitched. 'Some bird on her phone, having an argument by the looks of it.' She tilted her head back. 'A couple having drinks. Ooh look, look, he's making a move on her.'

'Let me see, let me see. Are they having sex?' Emma said, grabbing at the binoculars.

Hope brushed her hand away, lowered the binoculars, frowned, then lifted them for another look. 'Wait a minute.'

'What are they doing? Tell me.'

'Nothing. These lenses are shit. Everything's blurry. I don't know what your mum thought you'd see through them.' She spat out the words as if they made her physically ill.

'Well they wouldn't be state of the art on their budget, even if they'd bought them especially,' Emma said, retrieving the binoculars from Hope to look for herself.

Straight ahead, she caught a pair of dark curtains closing. *Too late!* She moved across to the next window and saw a mother sitting in an armchair, breastfeeding a child. *Boring!* Moving on, she settled on a window showcasing a large, sleekly furnished living room. Two women were sitting on a sofa. Emma gasped when one of them stood and began swaying her hips from side to side to unheard music. *Now this is what I'm talking about.*

Suddenly, she was very happy with her 'unusual' birthday present. As much as she wanted to lower her gaze, she remained transfixed by the window show. Lithe arms pulled the shirt over a dark head, bringing a slim torso and lace-covered breasts into view.

When Hope called from the living room, Emma reluctantly returned inside.

'They shouldn't have bothered giving you those.'

'I don't know. They might come in handy,' she said cryptically, her mind fixed on the dancing woman in the apartment across the road. She wondered if she was naked yet and giving her lover a lap dance. Emma was tempted to go and have another peek, but thought better of it. Wasn't this exactly what she had told Hope she didn't want to do? Hope would never let her live it down if she found out.

'Come in handy for what? Giving you an eye ache? If you want, I can flog them on eBay for you,' she said, switching on the TV with the remote control.

Emma laid the binoculars on the window ledge and went in search of the pizza menu. 'That seems a bit mean.'

By midnight, Hope had fallen asleep in the armchair. Emma rubbed her eyes, gathered the empty pizza boxes by her feet, and stood. She looked down at Hope and decided to let her sleep. Hope would go to bed when she woke up with a numb arm like she normally did when she leant on it for too long.

Emma did a quick tidy and was on her way back to her bedroom when she remembered she'd left the binoculars in the living room. Retrieving them, she headed back up the hallway. Despite her best intentions, she found herself at her window, looking out with her spyglasses at the apartments opposite hers.

'Oh well,' she said when she saw that the lesbian couple's curtains were drawn.

There's always tomorrow night.

Chapter Seven

What I need is a hot sea-salt bath and … yes, Lauren admitted to herself, *sex*. One drawback of single life was the lack of a warm body next to you. *And that's why the rampant rabbit was invented: for frisky, single women like me.*

Lauren padded down the hallway to the bathroom, stripping at the open doorway. She spied her nakedness as she passed the large mirror. Weekly kick boxing lessons had kept her in shape and the muscles in her slim arms were well defined. Bending over the bathtub, she turned the tap, releasing a gush of hot water, and sank the plug in the hole. As she poured in the sea salts, she heard the faint ring of her phone. She considered leaving it, but then remembered Frankie had said earlier he'd call to see if she wanted to go out for a drink. She hurried from the bathroom to the living room.

Snatching the phone from the sofa without looking at the caller ID, she said, 'Hello?'

'Ma belle, please don't hang up,' Fiona said quickly.

Lauren groaned. 'What is it, Fi? I've just got home. I had an interview today and I'm really tired.'

'I'm sorry, but we need—'

'Need? I thought you didn't need anything?'

'You know what I mean.'

'No, actually, I don't. As far as I'm concerned, you needed the freedom to fuck whoever you wanted. I'm sure you're making the most of it.'

'You know that's not true. I really am sorry. I overstepped the mark *once* and I've regretted it ever since. Je le jure,' she protested.

'Oh get real, will you? Regret isn't even in your vocabulary.' Lauren shivered. She glanced down, saw her pink nipples were fully erect, and locked her free arm over her chest.

That was the problem with exes. They were comfortable, like slipping your feet into a pair of worn slippers. No matter how much you knew they needed binning, 'what ifs' always played at the back of your mind. *What if I never find anyone else? What if I'm just chasing a dream and the perfect relationship doesn't exist after all?*

Right then, when she was feeling a sense of loneliness, it would have been all too easy to give in. To tell Fiona to fly over and welcome her into her bed as if nothing had happened. To carry on as if Fiona hadn't broken the bond of trust between them. It would have been easy, but not logical or even possible. Not now. An untraversable distance existed between them, preventing them from being together again.

'I want you to stop calling me. I don't want to have to change my number again.'

'So that's it?'

'That's it.'

'Over one meaningless shag?'

'Yeah.' Lauren hoped Fiona could hear the finality in her voice. This constant rehashing of apologies that changed nothing had grown tiresome.

'If you could put yourself in my shoes, you'd understand.'

Lauren unconsciously moved her hand to her throat. 'Are you seriously putting the blame for this at my feet?'

'I'm not saying it's all your fault. I'm saying it's not all my fault either.'

'Piss off with your psychobabble. Go and tell it to someone who gives a flying fuck.'

'I'll never let you go, Lauren.' Her voice was low and threatening.

'In this instance, you don't have a choice.'

For the second time in two days, Lauren hung up on Fiona. She quickly dialled Frankie's number and arranged to meet up with him. Her date with the rampant rabbit would have to wait. The comfort and security she desperately needed could only come from a bottle.

Chapter Eight

Although there weren't any lingering signs of the emotional stress evident in their last session, Emma studied Louise from across her desk, not totally convinced she was 'fine and doing great,' as she'd said when she arrived forty-five minutes earlier. Something other than family life was clearly bothering her, but Emma didn't know what the source of her concern was. Not yet anyway.

Louise's gaze darted around the room as she gnawed on her nails. Emma noted that Louise had shifted in her seat at least ten times to find a comfortable position. Now and again, she glanced at Emma then averted her gaze. Several minutes had passed since Louise last spoke, then suddenly, without looking up, she said, 'Do you think I'm gay because of what my uncle did to me?'

Emma rested her hands in her lap. The question didn't surprise her. Survivors of sexual abuse commonly asked this question, and it was difficult to answer, so she took a few seconds to respond.

'I don't know,' she said honestly. 'But let's look at it like this: if it were true, there wouldn't be any heterosexual female survivors of abuse.'

Louise grunted an agreement.

'And anyway, does it really matter whether you're gay or not?'

Louise grimaced and rubbed the back of her neck. 'Not really. It's not so much about being gay. It's about knowing where I belong. Where I fit in. Isn't that what everybody wants?'

Emma empathised with feeling like a square peg in a round hole. She had felt displaced her entire life. 'There's nothing wrong with being unique. There's no rulebook that says you have to be like everyone else. Imagine how boring life would be if we were all the same?'

'Suppose so. But what if I go with a woman and it feels wrong? Then what?'

'Louise, you're in control of your life and your body. Nobody can force you to do anything you don't want—'

'Unless they're bigger and stronger than me.'

'In which case that would be an assault. It's not the same as consent. If we can't fight back, that's not our shame to carry. It's the abuser's.'

'Do you think I should at least try and, you know, date men? To make sure it's the right choice?'

They were treading in muddy waters. Emma's interpretation of 'dating'—going to the cinema and grabbing something to eat after—was very different from Louise's, who was implying she wanted to have sex with men in order to find herself.

Emma crossed her arms over her chest. 'You're eighteen years old. You have the world at your feet. Trust yourself to know what you want without doing anything too drastic. And when you find yourself, accept who you are with open arms. Gay, straight, or even bisexual.'

'You forgot asexual.'

'Even that,' Emma said with a reassuring smile.

Outside, dark skies had replaced the daylight. As usual, she'd gone well past their allotted time, not that it bothered her. It wasn't as if she had anything—or anyone—to rush home for.

'Am I allowed to ask you a personal question?'

Emma nodded slowly, hoping it wasn't *too personal*. 'Sure.'

'The incident you told me about, the one at school with that girl. What do you remember most about her?'

'Her ears.'

Louise looked at her quizzically. 'Her ears? Why?'

In her mind's eye, Emma pictured Lauren's small, rounded ears that stuck out ever so slightly. 'Because I loved looking at them from behind when she wore her hair in a bundle on top of her head. They were the cutest ears I'd ever seen.'

A gentle tap on the door preceded Gina, her bespectacled manager, poking her head inside the office. 'We're getting ready to lock up, Emma.'

'Okay, won't be long.' She gave her a brief, apologetic glance.

Emma remained with Louise long enough to arrange their next appointment, and then she packed up for the day and made her way home. She stopped at the corner shop and bought a bottle of white wine, a large bag of toffee-coated popcorn, ready salted crisps, and a salsa dip. *I hope those women will be on view again.*

Emma wondered what Hope would say if she knew she had bought snacks for her dabble in voyeurism. She would probably be delighted that Emma had done something out of the norm.

Letting herself into her apartment, she kicked off her shoes and stooped to retrieve her mail. She sucked air through her teeth as she sorted through the letters. Junk, junk, and more junk. She tossed the mail onto the hallway table and hung her jacket on the knob.

Emma headed to the living room and turned on the TV for background noise. After spending the day listening to people's problems, she should have been happy with the silence living alone afforded her, but it only reaffirmed her single status. Maybe her dislike of solitude came from growing up as an only child—well, until Hope came along, but by then she was a teenager. Growing up, she had longed for a home full of fun and visitors, but it was never meant to be. After her father had died of a heart attack, the little energy present in Emma's life was sucked away. That was until her mum met Alex, but even then, her mother just wanted to make him happy.

Emma brushed her hair away from her face and stretched her arms above her head, loosening the tension in them. It was good to be home.

She walked into the kitchen, retrieved a glass, and filled it with a generous amount of wine. She deserved it after the long day she'd had. Opening the cupboard door, she took out a large wooden bowl and tipped the popcorn into it.

'Let the action begin,' she said aloud.

A hybrid of guilt and excitement built within as she entered her bedroom. Grabbing her binoculars from the side of her bed, she slid the balcony door open and stepped outside. A cool breeze gently caressed her face as she covered her eyes with the lenses. Hope had been right; the focus wasn't great, but who was she to complain?

She trained the binoculars in the direction of the couple she had seen last night but was met with darkness. *Yes, Emma, some people do have a life and actually go out in the evening.*

Unperturbed, she moved along the building until she came to the first window with any sign of life. She focused the lens on a dimly lit apartment a couple of floors below and frowned. *Why is the owner wearing a balaclava in his own home?*

Unless … Emma turned quickly, knocking over the wine glass balanced on the rail. 'Oh my God. Oh my God. No, you bastard! Stop! Stop!'

She ran from the room and grabbed her phone from her jacket in the hallway, then backtracked to the living room. Yanking open the door to the balcony, she stepped outside. Her fingers trembled as she dialled 999. Raising the binoculars while she waited for the call to connect, she traced the person's movements as they walked from the living room to the bedroom.

'I'm witnessing a burglary taking place right this second,' she said breathlessly to the emergency operator.

'Please hurry. They're in the bedroom. I don't know if anyone is home.'

'What's the address?'

'It's, um, oh crap.' She told the operator her own address. 'The apartment is in the block opposite me. I'm on the twenty-second floor and it's two floors below mine.' Even to her own ears she sounded panicked. She struggled to get her thoughts in order. 'The apartment is on the left-hand side of the building, on the very end. I remember now, it's called Braithwaite House. That's it. Please hurry.'

'An officer has been dispatched. Please stay on the line.'

'I will.' All she could hear was her ragged breathing. She felt sick to her stomach. *What if someone is home and the police don't get there in time?*

Time dragged on in slow motion. Police sirens blasted through the night air, drawing closer by the second. Emma kept her gaze on the intruder until the figure disappeared from view.

'Oh no. I think they've escaped,' she said into the phone. 'I can't see the person anymore.'

After another lifetime of waiting, the lights in the apartment came on. Two police officers moved around tentatively.

'The police are in the property,' Emma said, relieved that the problem was no longer hers to deal with.

'Okay. Please remain in your apartment. The officers will come by for a statement.'

Emma removed the phone from her ear and looked down at it, dumbfounded. *A statement? From me? Oh shit. They'll think I spy on my neighbours all the time.*

She went back inside, frantic with indecision. *Should I get rid of the binoculars? Okay, calm down and think about this. Oh crap.*

Half an hour later, Emma jumped when a loud knock sounded at her door. While waiting, she'd decided to tell the truth. *Okay, maybe not the part about hoping to see a bit of action, just that I was stargazing.*

She opened the front door and two burly police constables filled her doorway. They introduced themselves as PC Martin and PC Collins.

'Ms Clary?' PC Collins, the taller of the two, said.

'Yes. Come in.' She gestured for them to follow her into the living room.

'He was gone, wasn't he?' she said, forestalling the officer.

'How'd you know it was a he?' PC Martin asked, taking out a notebook and pen from the top pocket of his jacket.

'Um, I don't know for sure, but I've never heard of women going around in balaclavas and robbing places. They'd be no match for a man if they got caught.'

'You'd be surprised at who opportunistic burglars are. Can you tell me exactly what you saw?' PC Martin asked.

'Of course. Well, let's see. I arrived home around forty minutes ago and took my binoculars to see—' She stopped mid-sentence.

'To see?' PC Martin prompted.

'Um, to see the stars. I was a great fan of Patrick Moore when he was alive, so my mum and stepdad bought me a pair of binoculars to stargaze.' Emma knew she was rambling, but she couldn't help herself. 'So—'

'Did you see any stars?' PC Collins said with a look of amusement on his chiselled features.

'Well, no. It's quite cloudy tonight.'

The officers exchanged knowing glances that told Emma they thought she was a terrible liar. *The quicker I tell them what happened, the quicker they'll leave so I can put this break-in behind me.* 'What was I saying?'

'You were … um … stargazing,' PC Martin supplied.

'Yes, that's right. Anyway, I just so happened to, you know, be looking in the direction of the apartment in question when I spotted the intruder.' She glanced around the room, looking anywhere but at the officers. 'And the rest you know. I called the police and waited on the line with the operator until you arrived.'

'Did you notice anything specific about the intruder?'

Emma looked heavenwards and tapped her finger on her chin. 'Hmm, what can I tell you? Slim build. Stealthy looking. Moved around like a cat hiding from its unsuspecting prey. That's it, really. The light was quite dim.'

'Do you mind if I take a look for myself?' PC Collins asked, his hand outstretched towards her.

'Of course not,' she said and passed the binoculars to him. She watched as he disappeared beyond the balcony door.

'No one was at home, I hope,' she said.

PC Martin glanced up from his small notepad. 'No.'

'Thank God for that. How did they get in?'

'The lock was smashed.'

'I'm surprised no one heard anything.'

'When we arrived, cleaners were hoovering the stairwell. The noise from the hoover could have easily masked the sound of the break-in.'

'I see,' Emma said, running the tip of her finger along her jaw. 'Do you know who lives there?'

'One of my colleagues is tracing them now.'

PC Collins stepped back into the room with a grin on his face and shut the door behind him. 'Quite a bit of action going on out there. Lots to see if the clouds are buggering your chances of viewing the stars.'

Heat rushed to her face. The officers asked her a few more questions before leaving. Emma swore PC Collins had been smirking as he left.

That's it. First thing in the morning, those bloody things are going straight in the bin.

Chapter Nine

The telephone conversation with the police was shorter than Lauren had expected—not that they didn't ask all the right questions. They did and she answered them as best she could. They'd been in touch with the owner of the apartment, and Mrs Nook had arranged for the lock to be changed immediately. Due to the two large glasses of red wine in her system at the time, Lauren's reaction to the news of the break-in had been somewhat delayed. But now it was close to midnight and the effects of the alcohol were wearing off, as was her nonchalant attitude.

Lauren's fingers tightened around the wooden rolling pin as she walked from room to room, closing the blinds, checking in wardrobes and behind doors, and making sure no one was hiding in the shadows. She told herself the burglary was a coincidence and had nothing to do with her. It was London after all. Crime rates were at an all-time high, if you believed the mainstream media, so it must have been her bad luck. No matter what the case, a sense of uneasiness filled her. The one place in the world where she should have felt safe was alien to her. Someone had violated her space and touched her personal belongings. The thought made her skin crawl.

As far as she could tell, the burglar hadn't taken anything, but that didn't ease the wave of nausea gripping her.

Maybe I should call Fiona. For all her faults, Fiona was good at making Lauren feel protected. She took the phone from the bedside cabinet and ran her fingers over the keys. *It'll give her false hope if I call.* She pressed the mobile against her chest and closed her eyes. *I'm on my own. It's time I stopped using people as crutches.*

Normally if something spooked Lauren, like an overly familiar neighbour or if something didn't feel right, she would pack up her stuff and leave without looking back. That was one of the many benefits of working in the arts. As long as she had her camera, she could work from anywhere.

But she wouldn't run this time, especially since she didn't know if there was anything to flee from.

Lauren wanted to call Frankie but stopped herself. He'd been concerned about the break-in when the police contacted her while they were out. If he knew what a state she'd got herself in he'd want to come over, but company was the last thing she needed. She considered calling her mum again, but her mother had been near hysterical and on the brink of sending her dad around to look after Lauren after learning about the break-in. She couldn't ask that of her dad again, not after he'd given up so much of his time to babysit her in the past.

Lauren froze when she heard a noise in the passage. Common sense told her the intruder wasn't in the apartment—she'd made sure of that—but it didn't stop her overactive imagination from running rampant. The sound came again, only this time Lauren recognised the source: someone was knocking on her front door.

Tiptoeing to the door for fear of the visitor hearing her, she pressed her eye up to the peephole.

Shit! What the hell is Fi doing here?

'I know you're there, Lauren.'

She leant her head against the door. 'How did you get in the building?'

'I followed someone in. Are you going to open the door?'

'No, go away.'

'Not until I know you're all right.'

Lauren let out an exasperated breath. 'I'm fine.'

'At least open up so I can see for myself.'

Conceding that arguing with her was futile, Lauren reluctantly unbolted the lock and opened the door a crack.

'See, I'm fine,' she said.

Fiona's concerned eyes stared back at her. She inched forward. 'You look tired.'

'It's been a long day.'

'I 'eard about the break-in,' Fiona said.

'Jesus Christ. Is my mum still discussing my business with you?'

'Come on, don't be like that. Your mum wasn't gossiping. She said you sounded shaken. She's worried about you.'

'I told her I was fine. You know how she likes to exaggerate.'

'Look, I've come a long way, I jumped on the Eurostar as soon as I 'eard and came straight 'ere. Can you at least let me in? S'il te plait?'

Will this ever end with this woman? Why won't she leave me alone? 'No, Fiona. I didn't ask you to come here. I'm getting ready for bed.'

'If you like, I can sleep on the sofa tonight.'

'Why would I want that?'

Fiona looked at her challengingly. 'I know you, remember? You think it's starting again.'

'That's where you're wrong. If I thought that, I wouldn't have stuck around.'

'I'm really worried about you. I thought you'd 'ave called me when this 'appened.'

'What for?'

Fiona reached out to touch Lauren's face but Lauren tilted her head back. 'I'm not your enemy.'

'No, you're my ex who has a problem respecting my boundaries.'

Fiona's brows furrowed as if she were giving her statement some thought. Then she shook her head regretfully. 'Suit yourself. I'm 'ere for you if you need me.'

'Thanks, but like I said, I'm fine.' She closed the door and made her way back to the living room.

Looking around, Lauren wondered if she'd been too hasty in dismissing her. *What if the burglar comes back?*

Maybe she should have taken Fiona up on her offer to spend the night. Lauren flopped down on the sofa, fully clothed, and to her surprise, fell asleep in seconds.

Chapter Ten

Surrounded by three of her work colleagues, Emma took a moment to catch her breath before continuing her tale about the drama that had taken place the previous night. In the kitchenette area, where they were sitting around a small coffee table, two of her three colleagues looked at her with anticipation. Normally it was Gina who did all the talking during their end-of-day meetings, while Emma sat and listened with nothing to say—which was not surprising, seeing as she never went anywhere—but today the spotlight was on her.

'He was—'

'Hold on, hold on, hold on. How do you know it was a he if his head was covered?' Jack—a huge bear of a man with an explosion of black, curly hair—asked. His large eyes looked expectantly at her from behind bifocal glasses as he impatiently tapped a pen against the edge of the table.

Doubt crossed Emma's features. 'I don't. I just assumed.'

'Assumed? Am I getting a sense of gender discrimination here?' Jack said with humour.

'Point taken, Mr Rodgers,' Emma said, giving him a wink. 'I'll say "they", for clarity. And anyway, their gender is for the police to figure out.'

Wendy, who was reading a magazine while she ate a slab of cake, looked up at Emma contemptuously.

'Perhaps the police should be more interested in why *you* were spying on your neighbours with a pair of binoculars.'

Trust her to make this about me! Emma's jaw ached from clenching her teeth. 'I was not spying. For your information—'

'So what were you doing? Bird watching in the dark?' Wendy interrupted in a curt, mocking tone.

'I was … looking for UFOs,' she said, unwilling to face the reality of Wendy's accusation: that she was a peeping Emma. Was she? After all, she had been looking into the homes of strangers.

'Yeah, I believe you …'

Emma balled her hands into fists on her lap. Wendy was trying her patience. What Emma couldn't understand was why Wendy always homed in on her. Instead of behaving like an adult and telling her what the problem was, Wendy insisted on using passive-aggressive remarks.

'To be honest, I couldn't give a rat's arse either way—'

'Break it up, you two,' Gina reprimanded and wiped frosting from her mouth with a napkin. 'You're not in a school playground.'

'She started it,' Emma said pointedly. 'She's always poking her nose in where it's not wanted.'

'And you've always got your head in the clouds,' Wendy countered, removing her bronze-framed glasses to clean the lenses with a tissue. For a woman of fifty, she certainly enjoyed wearing clothes aimed at the more 'mature woman'. Wendy reminded Emma of a chemistry teacher rather than of a single woman with a healthy social life. According to most of her colleagues at the office, Wendy thought the 'mature look' made her appear sophisticated.

'Enough,' Gina said with finality. 'Back to your story, Emma. What was the last word from the police?'

'They said they were going to track down the resident.'

Jack gave an exaggerated shudder. 'That is so creepy.'

'What, someone spying on you with a pair of binoculars?' Wendy said, her voice dripping with sarcasm.

'No. The thought of some strange geezer going through a woman's knicker drawer and doing God knows what else.'

'Let's hope the police catch the creep, whoever it is,' Gina said.

'Here, here,' Jack replied.

'Thinking about it, maybe it was a good thing you were watching. You're like neighbourhood watch, but in the air. Imagine all the things you could see from your vantage point,' Gina said.

'Private things,' Wendy mumbled with thinly veiled scorn.

'Give it a break, Wendy,' Emma said. 'Your constant digging is getting boring.'

Ever since Wendy joined the company, the atmosphere had been the same. Her incessant needling of Emma was her favourite pastime. Lately, Emma had started to answer back, but it hadn't made the slightest difference. As far as Wendy was concerned, Emma was fair game.

'Oh, sorry. I'm the unreasonable one, am I? Since when is it okay to invade people's privacy? I swear the world's gone mad,' Wendy said with a shake of her head.

'Let's put this to bed once and for all, shall we? Yes, I was eyeing up people through my binoculars. And no, I shouldn't have been, you're right. I was out of order. Now either call the police or—' Emma stopped herself before she became unprofessional and swore at her. 'Just back off.'

'Touchy, aren't we?' Wendy said triumphantly.

'Only when it comes to you,' Emma muttered.

'Anyway, you have no idea who's living there?' Jack asked.

'No.' Emma picked up her coffee and took a sip.

A deep frown creased his forehead. 'You mean you didn't have a look this morning to make sure they're okay?'

'Uh no. Should I have?' The question was genuine. What if she witnessed something else she had to report to the police? Surely they'd be pissed off if the 'vigilante in the sky' kept snooping on her neighbours.

Jack's eyes grew distant. 'I think so. What if the intruder comes back? The resident could be in danger.'

'You think?' Emma said.

'Yeah, don't you?' Jack said as if he couldn't believe he needed to tell her such an obvious thing.

'I could always go round there after work to make sure they're all right, I suppose.'

'I would,' Jack said. 'It could be a little old biddy living there all by herself.'

Emma gasped. 'Oh no, don't say that.'

'I second that. Poor cow could be frightened to death knowing someone's been in her home,' Gina added.

'Lucky for her she wasn't in,' Jack said.

'Come on, guys, give it a break,' Emma said. 'We don't even know if this fictitious lady lives there. It could be a six-foot biker built like a brick shithouse for all we know.'

'Well you'll know soon enough,' Gina said. 'And when you do, cc us all in an email, won't you?'

'Don't bother with me,' Wendy said, flipping a page of the *Wedding Daze* magazine she was reading.

'Don't worry, I won't,' Emma said.

Wendy burst out laughing.

'Share the joke, then,' Jack said.

'Some people are so tacky,' Wendy said. 'There's an article on controversial wedding decisions. The worst so far is a bride's choice of wedding cake. This one chose a ginger bread cake. How tacky. Can you imagine the sight of an ugly brown sponge sitting in the middle of a beautifully decorated table? It beggars belief, doesn't it?'

'What beggars belief is your judgemental attitude. Does anyone escape your wrath?' Emma said.

'Is that the time?' Jack pulled Emma to her feet. 'Home for you. You've got a mission to complete, remember? I'll be eagerly checking my email for your update.'

Emma unhooked her coat from the back of her chair. 'Okay. If you don't hear from me by eight, you know someone's done away with me.'

'I'll keep my fingers crossed,' Wendy said, putting her specs back on her nose.

Chapter Eleven

Emma mentally rehearsed what she would say to the tenant. *I'm the one who called the police when I saw the intruder in your apartment.*

How could you see inside my place from all the way over there? she imagined the fictitious tenant replying.

How indeed.

'Just admit you were looking for cheap thrills,' she muttered under her breath, ashamed of herself. Maybe Wendy was right; maybe she was a pervert.

But the end justifies the means, she tried to convince herself—unsuccessfully.

'Hold the door,' Emma called out to the parcel deliveryman entering the building. He looked at her with impatience but waited until she was inside. She headed for the lift and he walked off in the opposite direction.

How will I explain without seeming like a nutter? No intelligent person would fall for her story about gazing at the stars, the police certainly hadn't. No, there had to be another way. The lift doors opened and she stepped inside. Pressing the button for the twentieth floor, she gathered her thoughts. *Okay, I've got my cover story. I'll say my binoculars were a present, which they were, and I was trying to see my sister coming up the road. Yeah, that sounds plausible.*

When the lift halted and the doors opened, Emma walked the hundred yards to the door she assumed was the right one. With her story straight in her head, she pressed the bell and waited. She heard footsteps, then silence. Imagining an elderly woman lying on the floor in a pool of blood, she rang the bell again, followed by a couple of knocks on the door.

'Hello,' she called.

The echo of her knock faded for the third time. There was still no answer, and she didn't hear any groaning or other signs of distress. Deciding the occupant didn't want to be disturbed, Emma turned to go. *At least I tried.*

Not five steps towards the lift, she heard the distinct sound of a lock turning and the creaking of a door opening.

'Hey,' a strong female voice said. 'Can I help you?'

Goosebumps exploded up and down Emma's skin. *That voice.*

No, it wasn't possible.

A knot of anticipation tightened in Emma's stomach. The world couldn't be *that* small. Emma turned towards the apartment, a fake smile plastered on her face. Her heart pounded as she tried to calm herself.

It'll be a complete stranger with an eerily familiar voice.

'Hi, sorry, I was …' Whatever she was going to say died on her lips. The woman leaning out of the apartment had blonde hair, but her face, though older and thinner, was unmistakable. Emma would know; she had been living with the vision of Lauren in her mind for most of her adult life.

'Lauren?' Her name emerged from Emma's throat

in a hoarse whisper.

The other woman's eyes widened. 'Do I know you?'

Her response punched Emma in the gut. Had she really changed so much in the intervening years, or was she just a fleeting memory from Lauren's past?

Emma walked back to Lauren, accruing time to compose herself.

Shock ricocheted in Lauren's grey eyes, and she let out an incredulous laugh. 'Emma? What the …? How?'

Emma's knees weakened, and she placed her hand on the wall, thankful for the support.

'I was going to ask you the same,' Emma said.

Lauren gave Emma a bright smile—the same smile she often remembered.

'Come here,' Lauren said, stepping out of her apartment, and wrapping Emma in a hug.

The feel of Lauren's body surrounding her and the familiar scent of the Jean Paul Gaultier perfume she wore made her head spin.

'What are you doing here?' Lauren asked as she pulled away, keeping Emma at arm's length. 'How did you know I was staying here?'

Emma blinked, some of her shock wearing off.

'Know you …?' Emma shook her head. 'I didn't. I live across the street. I came to check that the tenant who lives here was okay after the break-in.'

Lauren's eyes narrowed and she tilted her head. 'How did you know about the break-in?'

Emma stepped out of Lauren's hold, heat burning

her face. 'Because I reported it.'

'But how?'

'I'm your neighbour. I live in the block opposite you at number 2253,' Emma rambled as she prepared to launch into her rehearsed story. 'Anyway, I was testing out my new binoculars—'

Lauren's perfect eyebrow rose.

Emma huffed. 'They were a birthday present. I was looking out for Hope—'

'Hope's still living in London as well?' The caged looked in Lauren's eyes faded as disbelief coloured them.

The sight allowed Emma to take a breath and relax as she redirected the focus from her. 'Yeah, she lives in Elephant and Castle. So how long have you lived here? How have I not bumped into you before now?'

'Only a few days. I found this place on Airbnb. It's only for a little while. I'm here on business.'

'Oh.' Emma's joy plummeted. 'What's a little while?'

'A couple of weeks.'

'A couple of weeks?' The words came out high-pitched from the disappointment tightening her throat. That wasn't nearly enough time to reconnect. A blur of questions spun in her mind. How would she find out about the past fourteen years of Lauren's life in two weeks?

With a deep sense of foreboding, she asked, 'Then where?'

Oh God, please don't let her say some country that requires two planes and a boat ride to get to.

'Back home to Paris.'

'Paris, huh.' Emma did a quick calculation. *Paris, that's two and a half hours away. Well, three if you add on the time it takes to get to Kings Cross. That's not as bad as it could be. Fares are cheap enough.* She concluded her train of thought before she got carried away. Who said Lauren would even invite her over to visit?

Lauren jerked her head towards her apartment. 'Have you got time for a drink?'

'Sure,' Emma said, proud that her voice had sounded casual and confident, betraying none of the nerves assaulting her.

She followed Lauren inside the apartment.

'I just need to let my colleagues know you're okay. Well, not you specifically, but the person living here,' Emma said, taking her phone from her pocket as she walked down the hallway towards the living room.

'Wine? Tea? Coffee?' Lauren enquired.

'Wine would be great, thanks.' When Lauren disappeared through the doorway, Emma sat on the comfy sofa and pulled up her email on her iPhone.

> *Fear not. I'm fine. You won't believe it, but the tenant is someone I knew at school :-0*

She resisted the urge to write something insulting about Wendy and instead pressed 'send' and shoved the phone back into her pocket. Leaning against the cushion, still giddy with excitement, she took in the apartment with a sweeping glance. It was impressive, she decided. While the layout was the same as her own apartment, the interior design lent the space a different vibe. *Classy. Well put together by someone who knows what they're doing.*

The dark floor was expensive laminate, unlike the cheap crap she'd picked up at B&Q during a bank holiday sale. Noting the absence of bits and bobs hanging around, she thought about the state she'd left her bedroom in that morning and felt a little guilty. Everyone else managed to keep their homes spotless— except her. *I'll tidy up when I go home.*

As Emma slipped out of her jacket, a large, colourful canvas hanging on the wall drew her eye.

'Here we go.' Lauren entered the room, a glass of white wine in each hand. She passed one to Emma before lowering herself onto a multi-coloured rug, carefully balancing her wine in one hand.

'Thanks.'

'Gosh, the last time I saw you, you still had braces. Look at you now. You've grown your hair. That's why I didn't recognise you at first.' Lauren glanced at Emma's hand as she brought the glass to her lips. 'Not married?'

'Me? Oh no.'

Lauren looked at her with interest. 'Kids?'

'Does it look like it with a figure like this?' she joked. 'What about you?'

'Nope. Where would I find the time … or a man?'

Hmm, that's a bit of an ambiguous statement. Emma giggled. 'There is that.'

'So how's Hope?'

'She's doing really well. She runs her own web design business. Her latest client is *Wedding Daze*. She's building them a new site from scratch.'

The flicker in her eyes told Emma she was impressed.

'And you?' Lauren asked. 'What career path did you choose?'

'I'm a counsellor.'

'For?'

'Men and women who are trying to come to terms with their sexuality and all that comes with it. Finding the right way to tell family and friends, being out at work. That sort of thing.' *Bumping into the love of your life again and realising you haven't got the faintest idea what to do about it.*

Lauren rocked back on her heels. 'Really?'

'Yep. I work for the Living Well Foundation.'

Emma was proud to be part of the organisation. They provided a lot of help to vulnerable people. The founder, Janet Lewis, had opened the place in honour of her daughter who had committed suicide on her twentieth birthday in the early eighties. The harrowing letter she had left behind stated she couldn't see a future for herself in a world where there was so much hatred and anger toward people because of who they loved. Janet had spoken at Emma's university, and Emma was so moved that she volunteered to work for the charity while she obtained her degree in counselling. After she had earned her degree, Janet offered her a full-time job, and she hadn't hesitated to accept.

'It's not surprising you ended up doing something that involved helping people find themselves, especially after all the slack you took at school for being different.'

'Which would have carried on if it wasn't for you.' Emma sipped her wine. *Where the hell am I going with this? Why can't I just ask her where she disappeared to?*

Emma hesitated as the courage she was waiting for failed to materialise.

'What about you?' she asked instead. 'What path did life lead you down?'

'Oh here and there.'

'Care to be more specific?'

Sounding evasive, Lauren said, 'Um, photography.'

'Really?'

'Uh-huh. Here, let me refill that, unless you've got somewhere to be?' Lauren said, reaching for Emma's glass. Her fingers were smooth and cool as they overlapped Emma's and a tremor of pleasure raged through her body.

'No, no a refill would be great, thanks,' she said. Nothing in the world could have dragged her away from Lauren, even if her life had depended on it.

'So what kind of pictures do you take?' Emma asked when Lauren returned with her refilled wineglass. 'Wildlife? Buildings?'

'People,' Lauren answered and sat back down on the rug.

Emma watched the words form on Lauren's sensual lips and realised she had never wanted to kiss someone so much. The air rushed from Emma's lungs, and she had to inhale deeply to steady herself. *I hope she didn't notice.*

'What, like models?'

'No, just strangers going about their everyday lives.'

Her soft, affectionate tone made Emma feel as if she were floating on large, white, fluffy clouds in the clear blue sky. When Lauren stared wordlessly across at her, Emma wondered what would have become of them had fate not intervened. Would they have survived the trials and tribulations of their early and late twenties and still have been together today? Couples did it all the time. They met at school, married, had kids, and were still living happily together. Some couples, anyway. After all the time that had passed, there was so much she wanted to say … and so much she realised she couldn't say, except: 'So was anything valuable taken yesterday?'

'No. Mrs Nooks, the woman who owns the apartment didn't think so.'

'That painting looks valuable.'

Lauren followed her gaze. 'Believe me, it has no value whatsoever. I painted it myself.'

'You did?

'Yep. I brought it as a gift for Mrs Nooks as a thank you for letting me book on such short notice.'

'Lucky her. It's amazing.'

'Thanks.'

Talk about hiding your talent under a bushel. Was Lauren one of those talented artists who always viewed their work as inferior no matter how impressed everyone said they were?

'Is that why you left all those years ago? To find the Van Gogh within?' Emma was sorry she'd asked when a dark expression crossed Lauren's features.

'I needed to get away.'

'Sounds quite drastic. Don't tell me. You committed a scandalous crime and have been doing time,' Emma said to lighten the mood.

'If you don't mind, I'd prefer not to talk about it.' Her voice trailed off.

'Oh okay. I'm sorry.'

'Hey, you haven't said anything wrong. It's just a time in my life I'd rather forget, okay?' Lauren leant forward and placed her hand on Emma's knee, sending her pulse into a frenzy.

Is our kiss included in that statement? Silence settled between them, both women lost in thought.

The bell chiming was all it took for the atmosphere in the room to drop to a cold zero. Lauren's hand jerked and her wine spilt everywhere.

'Damn!' Lauren cursed, jumped up, and grabbed a tissue from the box on the coffee table. She mopped up the stains pooling on the carpet.

Puzzled by her reaction, Emma took a handful of tissues and joined her, swabbing at the damp carpet.

She glanced at the pale face of the woman kneeling

on the floor next to her. 'Are you okay?'

'Yeah, I'm fine,' Lauren said, her voice terse, and she flashed a small smile at Emma that didn't reach her clouded, grey eyes.

'I think somebody's still waiting for you to answer the intercom.'

Lauren looked at her in confusion, then smacked her forehead with the palm of her hand. 'The intercom. Yeah, right. Won't be a minute.'

Lauren nimbly leapt up and left the room. Emma gathered the used tissues and leant over the sofa to throw them in the bin. In her peripheral vision, she noticed a lone suitcase. *Whoa, she travels light for two weeks.*

Whenever Emma went on a two-week holiday, she always had at least two suitcases to accommodate her needs, which was a waste of time because she never got around to wearing most of her swimwear, clothes, or shoes. Instead, she usually managed with a vest, sarong, and sandals.

She righted herself in her seat as the living room door opened a few minutes later and Lauren walked in with a tall, well-built man.

'Emma, this is Frankie. Frankie, Emma.' Lauren waved a hand between the two people by way of explanation.

Emma rose and extended her hand to the interloper, taking in his startling blue eyes that smiled at her as he shook her hand.

'Nice to meet you,' she said.

'Likewise, Emma.'

The three stood in awkward silence. Despite his friendliness, Frankie's presence had unbalanced the mood in the room. *Trust someone to turn up just when things were getting interesting. Typical!*

Noting Frankie glancing at her now and again, Emma took the hint that he wanted to be alone with Lauren. She grabbed her jacket from the sofa and slipped her arms into it. 'I didn't realise the time. I'd better be off. Thanks for the drink.'

Lauren nodded toward Emma's full glass. 'But you haven't—'

'It's okay. I've got some, um, washing to do.' *Washing? You bloody idiot.*

'If you're sure,' Lauren said. 'I'll walk you to the door.'

Emma noticed, with a surge of happiness, the note of regret in Lauren's voice.

'Thanks. See you, Frankie.' Emma threw the farewell over her shoulder as she left the room.

'Bye,' he said.

Great. They'll be finishing the wine meant for us. Emma followed Lauren to the front door. 'It was so good to see you again, Lauren.'

'You too.' Lauren opened the door for Emma to exit. 'Tell Hope I said hello.'

'I will.' Emma hovered in the communal hallway. She was disappointed when Lauren failed to mention meeting up with her again and assumed she had her hands full with Mr Pretty Boy standing in her living room. 'Well, if you're ever at a loose end, drop by for a coffee or something—like tea,' Emma quickly added.

Lauren assessed her and then said, 'I might just take you up on that offer. It really was good to see you again.'

When the door closed, Emma fought the urge to press her ear against the oak wood in the hope of overhearing their conversation. Did she really want to hear Lauren making out with a man behind closed doors?

Not a chance in hell.

She got what she'd come for—no more and no less. That would have to do. *For the time being anyway.*

Emma pulled her jacket down and flipped her dark locks out from under the collar as she walked briskly towards the lift. Thoughts of Lauren kept her company all the way back to her apartment.

Chapter Twelve

'Oi, oi, what's going on between you two then?' Frankie asked, wiggling his brows.

Lauren looked at Frankie in surprise. 'Who? Emma? Nothing's going on. She's someone I knew at school.'

The sheer coincidence that Emma— 'her' Emma Clary—had been the one to report the burglary still perplexed her. The chances were unbelievable. What shocked her more were the intense feelings she still felt for her. How was it possible that she could not see someone for fourteen years and still feel exactly the same about her?

Frankie leant back on the sofa and put his brogues up on the coffee table. Mischief glinted in his eyes. 'Are you sure? The chemistry in the air suggested otherwise.'

'Positive,' Lauren replied, stopping the conversation about Emma dead in its tracks. She didn't want to discuss her with Frankie; she wanted to savour their meeting for later.

Frankie set his feet down and crossed his ankle over his knee. 'If you say so. Anyway, sorry to drop by unannounced. I thought you'd come into the gallery today and when you didn't turn up I was worried.'

Lauren exhaled. 'Sorry, I didn't get a chance. I had forensics here this morning.'

During her time with Emma, she had managed to push all thoughts of the burglary out of her head. Now

Frankie had replanted the reminder at the forefront of her mind.

'Ah okay. What did the police say?'

'They knocked on people's doors but no one saw or heard anything. It's just a matter of waiting to see what forensics come up with now.'

'Don't they have CCTV here? The place looks pretty secure.'

'No unfortunately not.'

Frankie shook his head. 'You really should have called me and let me know what was happening. I've been trying to get you on the phone all day and it just went straight to voicemail. I had visions of all sorts happening to you.'

'I know. I really am sorry. If the break-in wasn't enough to deal with I had to turn my phone off as Fiona kept calling. She even turned up on my doorstep last night.'

'No! Really? She came all the way from Paris?'

'Crazy isn't it? My mum told her about the break-in and she was acting like the concerned girlfriend. I told her where to go.'

Frankie chuckled. 'So there's definitely no way you two are getting back together?'

Lauren picked up Emma's full wine glass and placed her lips over the red lipstick stain. A rush of warmth flooded through her body at the thought of Emma's lips. 'Fiona? No way. It's been months since we broke up. I think she's only bothering me now because that other woman's dumped her. Obviously she'd never admit it though. Anyway, I'd know by now if I had any regrets.'

'And you don't?'

'None whatsoever.'

'Good,' he said heartily, then coughed. 'Not good, as such. I just mean I'm glad you've made up—'

Lauren waved off his explanation. 'Don't worry. I get your drift.'

'Okay then ... any chance of a coffee since I'm here? At least you'll have a man to protect you if that burglar tries his luck again.'

She glared at him. 'That's what I needed: a reminder that he might come back. Thanks!'

'You know me. I'll tell you the truth whether you want to hear it or not.'

'That's what friends are for,' she replied.

Frankie grinned. Lauren gave up; he was incorrigible.

'So do you fancy something stronger than coffee?' she asked.

'Depends on what's on offer.'

'Wine or whisky?'

'If those are the only choices, whisky will have to do.'

He pulled himself to his feet and followed her into the kitchen. Lauren rummaged through the cupboards, looking for a whisky tumbler, while Frankie remained in the doorway, leaning against the frame.

'So how come you met up with this—What was her name?'

'Emma?'

'Yeah, Emma. I thought you were being discreet?'

Finding the glass, she laid it on the counter and poured a generous measure of whisky. 'I was. It was completely coincidental.'

'How so?'

Lauren crossed over to the freezer and fished out a couple of ice cubes.

'Believe it or not, she was the one who called the police yesterday.'

She dropped the ice into the glass and handed it to him.

'Now I'm really confused. How could she have known?'

Frankie looked at her over the rim of his glass. He wouldn't let the subject go until she had satisfied his curiosity.

'She was looking at this apartment through a pair of binoculars.'

'Your friend's a peeping Tom? Nice.'

'Don't be silly. I think she was being nosey,' she said and steered him back into the living room. 'These apartments practically look into one another.'

He sipped his drink and winced. 'That's too bad. Whoever broke in could be staking out this block to see when the apartments are empty.'

'Well one more incident and I'm out of here.' Lauren jerked her head in the direction of the suitcase.

Frankie must have heard the fear in her voice, because he put down his drink and regarded her seriously. 'You know the offer to stay at my place is still open.'

'That's very sweet, but I need my space. Anyway, there's no point talking about it before it's happened. Let's not tempt fate, okay?'

'Okay.'

Lauren pulled her hair into a ponytail and tied it with the band around her wrist. 'Did you speak to the reporter I had the interview with yesterday?'

'I did indeed,'

'And?' Lauren pressed.

'And …' He paused. 'She was very impressed with your work. In fact, she was so overwhelmed that the magazine is going to showcase your work as their main feature.'

'Get away! Really?'

'Yes, really.'

'I don't believe it.'

'Believe it. It's time you had more faith in yourself. If all goes well at the exhibition, your work will attract a lot of attention.'

'As long as it's only my work, I won't have a problem. Besides, it's not that I don't have faith in my work, but you can never be sure what reporters might write.'

Lauren hadn't known how to take Mrs Preston's cold personality. She had asked straight-to-the-point questions, firing them at Lauren without mercy. She had even asked why Lauren refused to let the press print her picture. Without going into too much detail, she'd told her it was personal, hoping the austere woman would leave it at that. The way Mrs Preston had talked about her work, Lauren got the idea that she hadn't thought much of it.

'Will you be seeing Emma again?' Frankie asked, interrupting her reverie of the interview.

He sat down again, looking very comfortable and at ease. Lauren wondered how some people could make themselves at home wherever they went, whilst she always furtively glanced at the nearest exit. *Old habits die hard.*

She realised Frankie was waiting for an answer.

'I dunno. We didn't make any plans or anything.' *And why didn't I?* For starters, she didn't know what this coincidental encounter meant. It wasn't as if they could pick up from fourteen years ago when … *when what?* She kissed Emma because she had felt sorry for her. She had wanted people to stop bullying her. That was all. *So why have I never forgotten that moment if it was just a sympathy kiss?*

No, it had been more than that, and Lauren knew it; she just didn't want to accept it. If she did, she would have to admit her connection with Emma was something she had never experienced since. Well, until tonight, that was.

Why was she thinking like this? Nothing would come of her reconnecting with Emma. Having a normal life with someone was way out of her reach. But daydreaming stove off the days when her lonely existence convinced her she would be alone forever.

'She's a very attractive woman.'

A picture of Emma floated in her head. 'So I noticed.'

Frankie clasped his hands together as if she'd revealed a secret. 'Ah, so you did, did you?'

'Of course. But it's not as simple as that.'

'Now I am intrigued. Do explain.'

'There's nothing to explain. I'm here to do a show. In two weeks, I'll be going back to Paris to resume my life there. I don't have time for a relationship. End of.'

'Who said anything about relationships?'

'Forget I mentioned it. I'm not interested in … anyone.' Lauren took a long sip of wine out of Emma's glass to stop herself from saying anything more.

'Point taken. Can I ask you something personal?'

'Nothing's stopped you before,' she said.

'How do you do it?'

Lauren threw him a puzzled look. 'Do what? Not fall head over heels in love with gorgeous women?'

'No. Live with this dark cloud over you all the time.'

'Who says I do?' She suppressed the urge to take a deep breath. She didn't want to talk about her situation in detail, but she gave in at the desperate expression on his face. 'I try not to think about it. The fear, the thing that makes me want to dig myself a deep hole to hide in, fits me like a second skin. I accept that someone out there wants to harm me, and I do my utmost to ensure it doesn't happen.'

He looked at her imploringly. 'I want—'

'Please don't say you want to look after me, Frankie, because that's not what I need. When I'm in Paris, I live a next-to-normal life. It's coming back here that's caused my anxiety to kick in big time.'

'Fair enough,' he said and pushed himself to his feet. 'And this is the problem with alcohol. It goes right bloody through me. Mind if I use your loo?'

'Feel free.'

Lauren drained the remaining wine in the glass and refilled it. It was nice to have company, be it male or female. She ignored the niggling thought telling her she'd much rather have Emma sitting on the sofa than Frankie.

Frankie returned with an envelope in hand. 'This letter just came through the door with pizza delivery leaflets.'

She stared up at the envelope. 'It'll be for the owner. You can leave it on the side table.'

'Unless you share the same name as your landlord, I'm pretty sure this is meant for you. Look, it has your real name on it, Lauren.' He passed her the envelope.

She slipped her hand inside and pulled out the paper.

'My real name? Are you—' The words caught in her throat, and her eyes darted around the room. The once large space closed in on her and she couldn't breathe. A roaring sound assaulted her ears and spots danced in front of her eyes, making her think, abstractly, that she might faint. She gasped, trying to pull air into her starved lungs. She lunged forward, falling on all fours on the soft rug.

No! It can't be happening. Please, not again! When was he here? The invisible monster was back. Where was he now? The note was lying on the floor face up, the black words on the white paper taunting her:

Your lights are still on. Aren't you sleeping yet?

Lauren pushed herself into a sitting position, her back against the sofa. She gripped her knees against her chest protectively. Would she ever be safe again?

Speaking in a raspy voice, she said, 'I've got to get out of here, Frankie. He's found me.'

'Calm down. Breathe. Deep breaths. It's all right.'

Frankie ran to the front door, and she heard him open it. Crawling back onto the sofa, she waited with bated breath until she heard Frankie's familiar footsteps walk back towards the room.

'I've checked outside. No one's there.'

Lauren inhaled deeply to calm her erratic thoughts.

Frankie ran his hand through his hair, looking as frantic as she felt. 'Come on, get some stuff together. You're coming home with me.'

'No,' she said, thinking of the sleeping arrangements in Frankie's one-bedroom apartment.

'You can't stay here alone, Lauren,' Frankie said, pulling her to her feet and embracing her.

'I won't.' Lauren considered calling Fiona, bundling up her belongings, and fleeing back to Paris with her, but she couldn't abandon Frankie and the exhibition he had put so much work into. She was in a vulnerable position and risking her safety by staying there, but where else could she go and not have to speak about the unexpected turn of events? Unless … She thought of Emma and whether it would be brazen of her to turn up on her doorstep. *She did say to drop by.*

'Will you walk with me across the road? I'll go to Emma's for a while,' she said, drawing back away from him. Once Lauren was out of the apartment, she would feel safer. Her bewildered brain would clear, and she would be stronger when considering her next move.

'Of course,' Frankie said, searching around for Lauren's jacket.

As they emerged onto the street, the air held a menacing feel. Panic bubbled inside her when she noticed a car parked across the road under the street lamp. The driver, a man she didn't recognise, stared back at her. Was he the one who had put the note through her letterbox? Her hands shook as she sought out Frankie's arm. Just when she was about to point the man out to him, a woman flanked by three small children approached the car and got in. The engine started and they drove away.

Pull yourself together. She tugged at Frankie's arm and headed in the direction of Emma's apartment block. The street ahead was completely empty. Relief washed over her. Whoever had posted the letter was no longer around, not that she could see anyway. Nonetheless, she took comfort in Frankie's presence. She was safe for now, but tomorrow was another matter altogether.

Chapter Thirteen

Emma had been spying on Frankie and Lauren for ten minutes. Nothing was amiss. They were having drinks like normal friends. Somewhat bored by the scene, Emma popped into the loo for two minutes, and when she returned, it was to a scene that twisted her heart.

I knew it! I knew there was something going on between those two!

Lauren was in Frankie's arms. Emma could scarcely draw a breath as she watched.

He was holding her close like a long-lost lover reunited with his heart's desire. How cruel and unfair of fate to bring Lauren back into her life, only for her to witness this. It occurred to her that if she'd thrown her spyglasses away like she was supposed to, she wouldn't have seen any of this and would have been none the wiser. So, in essence, she only had herself to blame. Emma drew the curtains closed and threw the binoculars on the bed.

If she wanted entertainment, she'd stick to Netflix. Emma wrapped her arms around herself, suddenly cold. She cursed as she wandered aimlessly around the apartment, moving from room to room. *When did life become so goddamn boring!*

TV was crap; it was as if those in charge of programme scheduling thought most of the population had dementia and weren't aware they were showing repeat after repeat of the same programmes that hadn't been worth watching the first time round. Getting blind drunk was out of the question; the older she got, the worse her hangovers became. The last time she'd been on a bender with Kelly from work, it had taken a whole week for her to fully recover. God! She was becoming a boring, old spinster. *Next, I'll take up knitting!*

She tortured herself with the image of what her life would have been like with Lauren in it. They would be snuggled up together on the sofa, drinking hot chocolate with marshmallows floating on top, watching a movie. Or better still, they'd be in her candlelit bedroom, naked, their bodies hot and slick from their hours of adventurous lovemaking.

Hmm, now that would be nice. Nice? *No, that would be amazing! But that won't be happening any time soon. Not with Mr Pretty Boy to keep her company.*

She strode to the living room and switched on the TV. The thought of spending the next two days alone was more than she could bear.

Emma had just started watching *The Flash* when her buzzer rang. With little enthusiasm, she wondered who could be calling. It couldn't be Hope; she was out on the town with an old friend from school she'd bumped into earlier in the week. This left only a deliveryman wanting to gain access to the building. *Welcome to my exciting life!*

She picked up the intercom phone and pressed it to her ear. 'Hello.'

'Emma, it's Lauren. Can I come up?'

Emma jerked back as if someone had poked her in her ear. She stared at the receiver, convinced she was hearing things. *Oh my God, she saw me. She knows I was watching her and ... him! I can't open the door. I can't! I'll never live this down.*

'Emma?'

Why did I speak? I could have pretended I'm not here.

'Emma, are you there? Hello?'

A hint of desperation tinged Lauren's voice. Without a second thought, Emma pressed the release button.

'Sorry, there's something wrong with my intercom. Come up.'

Emma opened the front door and waited. Ten minutes passed without any sign of Lauren. Convinced she'd changed her mind, Emma grabbed the handle to close the door, when she heard footsteps rushing down the hall. Lauren finally appeared at her door, her face flushed.

'Lauren?'

'I'm really sorry to drop in out of the blue, but—'

Emma's smile collapsed into a frown at the sight of Lauren's trembling hand, and she steered her inside.

'What's happened? Are you okay? Did Frankie hurt you?'

Lauren met her gaze. 'Frankie?'

'Yeah, the bloke you—'

'No, no one's done anything to me.'

Lauren's cheeks were so flushed that it alarmed Emma. She put a hand on Lauren's arm. 'But you're breathless, like you've been running.'

'I have been. Up twenty-two flights of stairs.'

'Are you crazy? If I did that, you'd have found me on the fourth, strike that, second floor dead of a heart attack. Why didn't you use the lift?'

'Claustrophobic. Can't do lifts.' Lauren's lips turned up in a small, brief smile.

Blinking rapidly, Emma said, 'But you're staying on—'

'The twentieth floor. I know, it doesn't make sense.' Lauren paused and then said, 'But I have my reasons, believe me.'

No wonder she looks so fit with all that exercise. Hmm. Her stamina must be fantastic! She led Lauren down the hallway and into the kitchen.

'Sorry for landing on you like this. Frankie was leaving and I started feeling nervous, being in the apartment alone after, you know, the burglary.'

'I don't blame you. I only witnessed it and it scared the crap out of me. I know it won't make you feel any better, but burglaries in this area are rare. The security in these apartments is normally really good. Take your jacket off and sit down. I'll get you something to drink.'

'I hope I'm not disrupting your evening. If you had plans to go out—'

'Out? Me? Nah. Fancied a night in. I'm sure you know how it is. Busy all week and by the time it gets to Friday, you just want to chill out.'

Lying didn't come naturally to Emma, but it wasn't hard when the only other option was to make herself look like Billy No Mates. The last thing she wanted was for Lauren to think she was some kind of loner who sat at home every night spying on her neighbours with her binoculars.

Emma took the bottle of wine from the fridge and poured two glasses, handing one to Lauren. 'Hopefully this will help you relax.'

Lauren gave her a grateful nod and took a mouthful of wine.

'Have you eaten?' Emma asked, noticing how pale Lauren looked now that the flush in her cheeks had receded. She didn't have much in the fridge, seeing as she hadn't been shopping for a week—except for snacks—but she was sure there was an egg or two to make an omelette. 'I can rustle up something light if you'd like.'

Lauren took another gulp of wine. 'Thanks, but I had something earlier.'

They sat in silence at the kitchen table, and Emma studied Lauren, whose gaze was focused on her near empty glass. An air of unease surrounded her. She seemed so vulnerable and nothing like the woman she had been speaking to barely an hour ago.

'You know, if it'll make you feel any better, you can stay here tonight.'

Butterflies fluttered in her stomach as she anxiously awaited Lauren's answer. Emma cringed at her insensitivity. She shouldn't be excited about having Lauren in her apartment, given the circumstances that had driven her here, but she couldn't help it. Maybe it was because she knew that, in the long run, Lauren would be safe. Emma had no doubt security at her building would be increased, and whatever lowlife had sneaked into the apartment block wouldn't be able to break in again so easily.

Lauren expelled a quick, relinquishing breath. 'Would you mind? I don't think I can face going back there tonight.'

'Of course not.' Emma emptied the rest of the wine into her glass. 'I'm out of wine. Shall I pop to the shop and get another bottle?'

Lauren clutched Emma's arm as she moved to stand.

'No, don't leave,' Lauren said. She waved her hand before correcting herself. 'Sorry, but I'd rather not be alone.'

'Hey, it's okay. If you're feeling anxious, alcohol's probably a bad idea anyway.' She wondered what had happened to Frankie and why he had left her alone if she was this scared. Maybe he'd stormed out after they'd had an argument.

Emma walked over to the kettle and flipped the switch on. 'So that guy you had in your apartment—'

'Frankie?'

'Yeah, is he …' Emma stammered, searching for the words that wouldn't come out coloured in jealousy. Just because Lauren had kissed her years ago didn't mean she was gay today or had been back then. Lauren had her reasons for doing what she'd done, and her motive for kissing her was something Emma wanted to know more than anything.

'Is he what?' Lauren said, frowning.

'Your …'

'My?'

'Nothing. It's not important.' Emma was sure Lauren could hear her heart beating.

'He's not my boyfriend, if that's what you're thinking. He's my agent.'

Lauren didn't say it in a smug or showy way, but rather reluctantly, as if it was something she didn't share too often with people.

'Your agent?' Relief flooded through Emma. 'Why would you need an agent? Are you famous or something in Paris?'

'No. I sell a few photos here and there. Frankie also owns a gallery, and he's exhibiting my work.'

'Wow, that's really something.'

'It's no big deal. Emma, would you mind if I had a look at my place with your binoculars?'

'Not at all. I'll have to remember where I put them. It's not like I make a habit of spying on people,' she jested as she abandoned making the tea and walked down the hallway to her bedroom. She dropped on the bed and grabbed the glasses, letting a few minutes pass before returning to the kitchen. Not finding Lauren, she went in search of her and found her standing in the living room in front of the window, peering out into the darkness.

'Ready?'

Lauren looked over her shoulder and Emma thought

she glimpsed real, unadulterated fear in her eyes. *Jesus, that burglary did a right number on her.*

Emma opened the door to the balcony and gestured for Lauren to step out first. Lauren took the binoculars from her and lifted them to her eyes.

'If you want a bit of live action, look to your far left.'

Lauren's eyebrow rose a fraction. 'So that's what you've been getting up to.'

Despite the cold air, heat crept up her neck and spread across her face. 'No. I just accidentally—'

'Is there such a thing as accidentally?'

Shifting her weight from foot to foot, she said weakly, 'Well, I kind of accidentally met you again, didn't I?'

'Yes, you did.'

'So can you see anything unusual in your apartment?' Emma asked, deflecting the conversation away from her peeping Tom habit.

'No. I know it's a bit cold, but can we have our tea out here?'

'Not a problem, if you like sitting around in arctic conditions.'

Lauren lowered the glasses and looked deeply into Emma's eyes, sending her heart racing again. 'Do you mind?'

'Of course not.' Emma fought to maintain her composure. All she wanted to do was grab Lauren by the hand and hold her hostage in her bedroom. 'I'll be two ticks.'

For the rest of the evening, over numerous cups of tea, Emma attempted to take Lauren's mind off the burglary. Her efforts appeared to be working, because Lauren gradually lessened the amount of time she spent looking over at her apartment, until she barely looked at all, preferring to engage fully in the conversation about their lives. They spoke about work, parents, the economy, UFOs—everything but that infamous kiss. Emma couldn't bring herself to mention it. *Does Lauren even remember?*

When the temperature dropped another few degrees, Emma suggested they go inside. Exhaustion washed over her bones like a warm tide, and her eyelids drooped as she struggled against sleep.

'I'll show you to the spare room,' Emma said, wishing Lauren were spending the night in her bed. Not in an intimate way, though she wouldn't have turned down the opportunity. Rather, she wanted Lauren to feel secure knowing someone was close by.

'I really appreciate you being here for me tonight.' Lauren self-consciously pulled on the end of a lock of hair.

'Looks like we're even,' Emma joked, hoping that by hinting at the kiss she wasn't overstepping her mark.

Lauren stepped a foot closer, gently kissed her cheek, and walked over to her bed.

Emma closed the door and put her hand to her face, where she could feel the heat from Lauren's lips. An hour later, Emma was sleeping peacefully, and for the first time in years she was content with her life.

Chapter Fourteen

Despite Gina calling Emma into work on a Saturday for an emergency meeting, Emma ran, skipped, and hopped her way there. She still couldn't believe it. Lauren was in her apartment, in her bed. Okay, technically she was in the spare room, but she was under her roof, breathing the same air as her. She made a mental note to never wash the bedding in that room again. She was happy, happy, happy, and nothing, or anyone, could burst her bubble. Not even the knowledge that Lauren was back for a short while or that they hadn't spoken about the elusive topic of why she had disappeared. Not even—

Oh God. Why would Wendy be the first person I see today?

Emma tried her hardest to hold on to her ebullient mood—even when Wendy cornered her in the corridor.

'Why does drama always follow you?'

'Wendy, I'm afraid you're out of luck today. Nothing you say or do will wind me up,' Emma said as she whirled past her.

Wendy shot her a mean grin. 'Let's see if you're still smiling once you've spoken to Gina.'

Any other day and the urge to wipe that grin off Wendy's face would have been paramount in Emma's mind, but today, it didn't even touch her.

Unfastening her jacket, Emma hurried to Gina's office. She waited a few seconds before knocking. If Wendy's happy demeanour was anything to go by, she was walking into the firing line for some wrongdoing. Exactly what she could have done wrong was a mystery to her. *No doubt I'll find out soon enough!*

She tapped on the door with the back of her knuckles.

Five excruciating seconds later, Gina answered, 'Come in.'

Even without seeing her face, Emma could sense the tension in her voice. As she entered, Gina dropped the telephone receiver back on its cradle and scratched the back of her head.

'I'm sorry to call you in at the weekend. Take a seat,' she said, indicating the leather chair in front of her walnut desk. Gina remained standing, which Emma recognized as a bad sign.

Emma lowered herself into the seat, her eyes never leaving Gina's worried face. 'What's wrong? Are you firing me?'

Gina laid the tip of her fingers on her desk and leant forward. Dark, unfathomable eyes that didn't once blink looked down at her. 'No, but I do have some bad news. It's about Louise.'

Emma involuntarily jerked forward. The hairs on her neck rose, her mind jumping to the worst possible scenario. 'Did someone hurt her?'

A ball of fear tightened in her stomach, nauseating her. Would the friends who'd told Louise that she needed fixing actually resort to violence?

'Yes. She was attacked last night. Sexually assaulted by a man.'

Her fingers splayed across her open mouth. 'Oh my God, no.'

'I'm afraid so.'

'Is she okay? I mean, is she in the hospital? Have the police been informed?'

Gina's broad shoulders sagged. 'No. She refuses to go to the hospital, and she doesn't want the police involved.'

'What!'

Gina slowly nodded, defeat written in her eyes. 'I know, I know. I was equally outraged, but it's not that simple. Seems Louise invited the him over to her house while her parents were out. Thank God they came back early and walked in while the assault was happening, but …'

'But what?'

'Louise's dad gave the young man a battering.'

'Jesus Christ. Poor Louise,' she choked out. Not only would Louise be traumatised from the sexual assault, but she would also have to face her father being arrested if the man pressed charges. Not that she could see that happening given the circumstances.

Gina eyed her warily. 'I know. It's heart breaking.'

Emma rubbed her hands over her face, feeling the need to do something practical. 'Is there anything I can do to help?'

'No, I'm afraid not.'

Emma closed her eyes and tilted her head back. 'I can't get my head around this.'

'Look, take Monday off. Have a long weekend.

Clear your mind.'

Emma opened her eyes. 'Do you think I should go and see her? Give her some support?'

'No, you mustn't do that under any circumstances. Her dad made it clear that he doesn't want anyone from this place anywhere near her.' Gina paused before adding in a softer voice, 'Especially you. I'm sorry.'

Emma rested her head in her hands. 'Oh great. So her parents think I had a hand in this.'

'They're understandably upset and are lashing out.'

'I should go and see her. If I could talk to her, even for a minute—'

'No, that is not to happen,' Gina said resolutely. 'And if you go against my order and the wishes of her parents, it will have a very big impact on your job here and any future one you might try to get.'

Emma shook her head a little as if to clear it. 'Are you threatening me, Gina?'

'No. I'm impressing upon you the seriousness of this situation and the potential penalties you will face if you don't comply with the parents' wishes.'

Something in Gina's tone told her that the friendly advice of taking Monday off wasn't advice after all. *Now there's a surprise!*

Gina was not concerned about Emma's emotional welfare; she wanted Emma out of the way. *In case Louise's father comes looking for me.*

Emma thought back to her last conversation with Louise. Nothing stood out. She didn't think she'd given bad advice when Louise had asked about men. At least

Emma hoped she hadn't. Then another thought struck her: Louise was going through all this alone. If what she'd said about her parents not being supportive was true, they might blame Louise for bringing this situation upon herself. *That poor, poor girl.*

'I thought this job entailed caring about our clients, not abandoning them in their hour of need,' Emma sputtered, bristling with indignation.

'It does. But it's also about knowing when to step back. If Louise wants to see you, I'm sure she'll find a way. The ball's in her court, and there's nothing more you can do. Are we clear on that?' Gina stared down at her, her eyebrows raised to emphasize the question.

With each ticking second, the decision weighed heavier on Emma's mind.

Standing, she said, 'Yes, okay, I get it. I think I will take Monday off. Will you let me know if you hear anything else?'

'Of course I will. I know it's hard, but try not to dwell on it.'

'That's easier said than done,' she said.

Emma's heart and head were pulling her in opposite directions. She knew Gina's stance was the right one and that if she crossed the line Gina wouldn't hesitate to follow through on her promise. The problem with working with vulnerable people was that she sometimes allowed her emotions to cloud her judgement. On one hand, it made her better at her job, because it enabled her to reach her clients on their level. On the other, when situations like this arose, she found it difficult to step back. She wanted to rush to Louise's side and protect her and prevent anything bad from ever happening to her again.

Emma walked out of Gina's office as if she'd told her the world was ending. Head bowed, she saw out of the corner of her eye the pleased smile on Wendy's face.

She flashed Wendy a look of disdain. *Why is the world so full of sad, messed-up people?*

***

The journey home could not have been more different than the one to work. It took all her mental energy to talk herself out of going to see Louise. She pictured the girl alone and scared with no one to talk to. What added salt to the wound was the fact her parents hadn't taken her to the hospital, where she would have received some degree of comfort and understanding.

Emma pushed open the front door to her apartment and was surprised to hear the sound of the TV. She poked her head in the living room. Empty. Then she heard a drawer banging shut in the kitchen.

'Lauren, I didn't expect you to still be here,' she said, slightly bewildered when she found Lauren stirring the contents of a mug on the counter. The moment was bittersweet. Under normal circumstances, she would have been ecstatic to find Lauren in her apartment—half of her was thrilled about it—but the thought of what Louise was going through cast a cloud over everything.

Lauren jumped and dropped the spoon on the

counter, almost spilling her beverage. She turned to Emma, her face ghostly white.

'Sorry,' Emma said and slipped out of her jacket. 'I didn't mean to spook you.'

Lauren took a deep breath and slowly released it. 'It's okay. I'm just a little jumpy. I saw your note about going into work. I was just having a coffee before I left.'

'Don't rush out on my account. You're more than welcome to stay here if you're not up to going home yet.'

'I have to face it sooner or later. Can I get you anything before I go?'

'Valium and lots of it.' Emma pulled a chair back from the table and slid into it. Although she was joking, after hearing about Louise's plight, she was sorely tempted to dull her heartache with pills, even to give herself an hour's respite from the overwhelming guilt.

'What did they call you into work for? Did something happen?'

Emma leant forward and dropped her forehead on the table with a thud. 'It did.'

'Whatever it is, it can't be good news by the look on your face.'

'No, it's not good. In fact, it's dreadful.'

After a few strained seconds, Lauren said, 'I haven't got anywhere important to be. Do you want to talk about it?'

'I can't. It's confidential.'

'Can I at least make you a drink?'

Sensing Lauren's scrutiny, Emma lifted her head

an inch to look at her. 'No thanks. Just having company is doing me the world of good.'

'Look, do you want to get out of here for a while? If you want, I can give you an exclusive preview of my exhibition?'

Emma jerked back into a sitting position. 'For real?'

Lauren nodded.

'In that case, lead the way.'

Though Emma was glad for the opportunity to peek into Lauren's life, the distraction couldn't last forever. She needed to find Louise and talk to her as soon as possible. The question was: How could she do that without jeopardising her job?

Chapter Fifteen

Lauren had spent the night tossing and turning, her mind frantic with fear and concern for what the future held for her, both personally and career wise. By the time dawn had risen over the city, she knew she had to stay in London despite her anxiety. Her exhibition was the opportunity of a lifetime, and there was no way she would throw it away.

Though anxious, Lauren tried to act as normal as possible. Whatever stress had befallen Emma at work, she didn't want to add her worries to the mix. She glanced at couples holding hands or embracing as the taxi carried them to their destination, and it saddened her to think of all the good times she might have missed out on with Emma, all because a stranger had taken it upon themselves to target her and send her into hiding.

As Lauren glanced sideways at Emma, she knew, given half a chance, she would take things further with her. Something about her just clicked and felt right. Lauren hazarded a guess that the feeling was mutual. She'd have to be blind not to see it in Emma's eyes when she looked at her. But it would be a big mistake to get involved with her romantically, especially with history repeating itself.

Lauren thought about the letter that had arrived yesterday, and her stomach knotted. Fear was a noose around her neck, and it would be the same for anyone close to her.

No, Emma's got her own life. Don't start messing with her. You'll only hurt her. She had to think with her head. *Don't go dreaming of the impossible.*

Her stern advice did nothing to stop the warm little globe of hope from lodging in her heart as Lauren watched Emma's brandy-coloured eyes flash with humour as Emma pointed out a cute dog poking its head out of the car window next to them. Lauren smiled in return and promised to enjoy the moment for what it was and not build castles in the air.

Emma's phone rang and she answered the call. The look of concern gradually faded from Emma's face after speaking with the caller for a couple of minutes. By the time she hung up, it was obvious the call had been a positive one.

'Good news I take it?' Lauren asked.

Emma nodded. 'Not as such. My boss was just checking up on me to see if I'm all right.'

By the time the taxi dropped them off outside the gallery, Lauren had learnt more about Emma's job and colleagues. They all sounded like a sincere bunch of people, except for a woman called Wendy. The way Emma had described her, she sounded like the last sort of person who should have been working in a customer-facing role.

Lauren led the way up to two large glass doors with 'Cotes House Art Gallery' printed on them in flowing letters.

'How chivalrous of you,' Emma joked when

Lauren opened the door and stepped aside to allow Emma to enter first.

'I try my best,' Lauren said and gestured for Emma to walk straight ahead.

To Lauren's surprise, the gallery was empty. At that time of day, she'd expected to see Frankie and his staff frantically getting the place in order. Tables and chairs were piled in the centre of the room. Unopened boxes were laid out on the floor, blocking doorways. The place was a mess, which was totally out of character for Frankie.

Emma let out a low whistle as she eyed the framed images on the wall. 'Are these yours?'

'Yes,' Lauren said.

'Very impressive. I can see why you're the star attraction.'

'I don't think people will be coming to see me, just my work.'

Emma stopped before a photo of an elderly man and woman sitting on a bench in the park. The craggy faces looked like they could have told a thousand stories. Next to them a young teenage couple sat, wrapped in each other's arms, oblivious to the world around them. The photo was in black and white, making the contrast more striking. The image mesmerised Lauren, even now.

Lauren pointed out the printed title below the photograph. 'Alpha and Omega - The Beginning and the End. That young couple doesn't realise that the elderly figures sitting just a few centimetres away could be them in several decades. That's not the way we look at things though, is it? We like to think we won't become some tragic figure, that it'll always be someone else. Then it happens to us and we realise we weren't that invincible after all. Life will get us, no matter how hard we evade it.'

Emma frowned. 'Yes it's sad when you think about it. That's why we have to make the most of our lives now and not worry about things that may or may not happen in the future.'

Lauren turned to look at her and smiled. 'Is that directed at me?'

'You've got to let this intruder business go. It'll drive you insane if you don't.' Emma lightly stroked Lauren's forearm.

'There's more to it than that.'

There wasn't any point in keeping the truth from Emma any longer. If she didn't tell her, Emma would no doubt think she was obsessing over nothing.

Lauren needed air, and the controlled temperature in the gallery was making it hard for her to breathe. 'Let's get out of here.'

'Huh? I want to see the rest of your work. That's why we're here, isn't it? To look at your exhibition?'

'There's something I have to tell you. It's about—'

'Vikki,' Frankie said from behind.

She turned around to see Molly and Frankie exiting his office. Molly gave her a quick wave as she headed for the exit and Lauren waved back. 'Hey, Frankie.'

Emma glanced from Lauren to Frankie, then back to Lauren.

'I didn't think I'd be seeing you today, you know, after—' Frankie said as he neared.

'I thought I'd bring Emma over and show her my work,' Lauren cut in.

'Oh yes, your old friend from school.' The disdain in his voice did not go unnoticed, and Emma's forced smile was evidence of her true feelings.

'Will this place be ready in time?' Lauren asked, gesturing around the room.

Frankie followed her gaze. 'Yes. There was a mix up with the employment agency. I've been on the phone with them, and I have a crew coming tomorrow to get things shipshape.'

'Okay, but if you need my help, let me know. We'll let you get on with it, shall we?'

'No.' Frankie stepped forward to block her way and placed his hand on her shoulder. 'Now that you're here, stay. I've got a few things I need to discuss with you.'

'We have plans. Can I call you later?' Lauren wanted to get out of the gallery. She was feeling closed in by the chaos surrounding her.

'No, not later, now. I'm sure your *friend* can look after herself while we talk,' he said with all the warmth of an iceberg.

Lauren opened her mouth to object but changed her mind. She was forgetting why she had returned to London. Frankie wanted to talk business, and that was what she was here to do. She turned to Emma, silently asking her if it was okay that she excuse herself to talk with Frankie.

Though her jaw was tense, Emma nodded. 'I'll be all right. I'll immerse myself in your work.'

'If you're sure.'

'Go on,' she insisted. Emma flashed Frankie a humourless smile and turned back to the photo of the two couples.

Following Frankie to his small office, she closed the door behind her. In a low, angry voice, she said, 'What the hell was that about?'

In all the years Lauren had known Frankie, she had never seen him act so rudely. He had even kept his cool on numerous occasions in Paris when a buyer had spoken down to him. As a rule, Frankie did not lose his temper—ever.

'What?' he asked innocently and slipped into his seat behind his desk.

'Out there. All of the emphasis on "friend". The hostile looks.'

'Can you blame me? I'm looking out for you and this is how you treat me? As if I'm the enemy when it's *her* you should be worried about?'

'What're you talking about?'

'It's obvious, isn't it? Your friend, *Emma*.' His voice dipped heavily on her name.

Lauren frowned. 'What about her?'

'Don't you think it's a bit strange that your "friend" finds you by looking through a pair of binoculars on the same night your stalker reappears?'

A short laugh escaped Lauren's lips. 'Have you gone mad? You think Emma's the one who sent me that letter?'

He leant back in his chair and lifted his chin defiantly. 'Yes, I do.'

'Well, you're wrong. Why would she do something like that?'

'So you would play right into her hands, which you did straight away.' When she remained silent, he continued. 'Think about it. As soon as you got the letter, what did you do? I'll tell you what you did. You went running straight over there as if she were some great protector.'

His eyes gleamed with anger.

'You're being ridiculous, and you know it. Emma and I—'

'Are just friends. Yes, so you keep saying.'

'And friends don't hurt each other. If she wanted me all to herself years ago, why would she have done something that sent me into hiding in another country?'

'Who said she was the original stalker?'

'Then that's where your theory falls apart, I'm afraid. Emma has no idea why I left for Paris, not yet anyway.'

His tone softened. 'All I'm saying is be careful of who you trust.'

'Does that include you?'

'No, Lauren. I'm your real friend, someone you can trust with your life.' His dark, thick eyebrows knitted together, belying the sentiment of his words.

'I appreciate that, Frankie. I really do. But I've got to go. I'll call you later.'

All the talk about her stalker was freaking her out. For all she knew, Frankie could have been the one to write the note. He'd had ample opportunity to slip it in with the pizza delivery leaflets and pretend they'd come together. The thought was as ludicrous as Frankie blaming Emma, and therein lay the problem; her stalker could be anyone.

She found Emma on the opposite side of the gallery, in front of a photo of a woman looking longingly at a pregnant woman.

'Do you mind if we leave?' Lauren said, a deep weariness overcoming her.

'Okay, but these images are—'

'I mean now,' Lauren said and headed towards the entrance.

Emma quickened her pace and caught up with her. 'Are you okay?'

'No, I need some air.' Lauren pushed the doors open and inhaled the fresh air deep into her lungs. She took a few steps along the pavement and then leant back against the gallery wall, closing her eyes to stop her senses from swimming. *When will this ever end?*

'Lauren, or should I call you Vikki? What the hell is going on with you?' Emma's concern penetrated through her thoughts, and Lauren opened her eyes to see Emma looking at her intently. 'Do you suffer from panic attacks?'

Lauren pushed off the wall, willing her heartbeat to slow. 'Can we talk when we get to your place? I need to get somewhere I feel safe.'

***

'So let me get this straight,' Emma said incredulously as they sat on the sofa together. 'Someone was stalking you at school? Jesus Christ, do you know who it was?'

Hearing the compassion in Emma's voice unleashed the memories from the mental dam she had erected. 'No idea. That's why I started using the name Vikki when I became a photographer. I couldn't make my name public.'

'What did they do to you?'

'It started off with notes on my parents' car windscreen. Stupid comments like, "I know what you did last Tuesday". Then I started receiving photographs of me in my house, in my bedroom, in the bathroom. I also had coffin brochures delivered to me with blank sympathy cards.'

'Oh my God, you must have been so frightened.'

'I was, so were my mum and dad. We kept everything I was sent and took it all to the police, but they didn't take my claims seriously. They had the gall to blame it on my looks. An officer even said, "It's normal for a lad to retaliate when a girl as attractive as you knocks him back."'

Lauren paused. She hadn't realised how raw she still felt about the policeman's dismissive comment.

Recounting the rest of the police interview was difficult, but she told Emma how the police officer had dismissed the notes as nothing, even when the wording and photographs were an obvious invasion of her privacy and proved that someone was following her wherever she went. He'd claimed there was nothing the police could do until the alleged stalker actually harmed her.

Tears welled in her eyes as she recalled seeing her dad cry for the first time in her life when he realised he was powerless to help her.

'So the next day, my dad bought me a one-way ticket to Paris to live with his sister, and that's where I've been ever since.'

'I really am speechless. I am so sorry that happened to you, Lauren. You are so strong.'

'No, I'm not. I didn't have a choice in the matter. Believe me, I'd rather be weak than have gone through all that. The whole experience has scarred me.'

Emma glanced up at the ceiling then back at Lauren. 'And you have no clue at all about who it might be?'

'No. That's what makes it ten times worse. It could be anyone.' Lauren dropped her head in despair. 'Everyone feels like a threat to me, you know?'

'And do you think the person who sent you the note yesterday is the same person who stalked you at school?'

'It must be. I've never received anything in France but every year since I left my parents have had "gifts" delivered to their house on my birthday. That's how I know the person hasn't gone away or given up.'

'Have you run into anyone you know since you returned to London?'

'No.' Lauren ran her fingers through her hair. 'Hold on a minute, yes. Mike, Mike what's his name from school?'

'Creepy Mike Foster?' Emma asked.

'Yeah, him.'

'Where did you see him?'

'Outside my apartment building.'

'Well it's got to be him then. It's a bit of a coincidence, isn't it?'

'I suppose, but where does that leave me? I don't have any proof it's him.'

'You should report it to the police.'

'No way. Not again. Not after the humiliation I suffered last time,' she said with a sour note.

'Things are different now. Give me a minute.' Emma left the room. She returned shortly after with her laptop and booted it up. She put it on the coffee table and sat next to Lauren.

Emma waited for the homepage to load then typed 'stalking laws UK' into the search bar. 469,000 hits came up. She scrolled down the page.

'There you go,' she said, clicking on a BBC news link. She read aloud from the article. '"New laws were introduced in 2012. The new offences created under the Protection of Freedoms Act means a charge can be brought when an alleged stalker's behaviour causes serious alarm or distress."'

'What will I say to the police? That a letter asking if I'm asleep caused me distress?'

'It did, didn't it?'

She clasped her hands on the sides of her face. 'Yes, but I'd feel stupid taking the letter to them. I know what you're saying about things changing, but I can't forget how pathetic the police made me feel when I went to them.'

'I understand where you're coming from,' Emma said, 'but it has to be an option. Have your parents kept everything they've been sent over the years?'

'Yes, I think so.'

'Well there you are, that's even more evidence. Maybe the police will pay Mike a visit and scare him off. Hang on, let's see what we can find out about him.'

She brought up Facebook and typed in Mike's name. In a split second, his page appeared.

'I know I shouldn't be judgemental, but look at his profile picture—he's still creepy,' Emma said and clicked on his employment history. 'Here you go. He works at Tesco in Lewisham.'

Lauren leant forward and stared at his picture. She had to admit, it wasn't very flattering, but that wasn't what caught her attention. His eyes—they were dark, almost black, as if he had no soul.

'I'll also see if he's on the electoral roll and we can get his address.' After a few minutes of searching Emma looked up from the screen. 'Damn, doesn't look like he is.'

'Not to worry, at least we've got somewhere to start.'

'I'd bet my life he's responsible, Lauren. You've got nothing to be afraid of,' Emma said.

Did Lauren dare believe Emma was right? That Mike would reveal himself as her stalker after all these years? It was at least something to consider. What else could she do? She was fresh out of ideas.

'What do you suggest we do?'

'We go to his workplace and confront him. Tell him if he doesn't leave you alone, we'll inform his manager what he's been up to.'

'And you think that will do the trick?'

'Look at it this way. When he was stalking you at school, he didn't have any responsibilities. Now he has a job and he lives in a shared house by the looks of it, which tells me he has rent to pay. Do you think he'll want to lose his job over a prank?'

'Okay, we'll go and see him,' Lauren murmured.

Emma drew her against her chest in a warm, comforting embrace.

Barely two hours ago, Lauren had promised not to get emotionally involved with Emma, and here she found herself in her arms and enjoying it thoroughly. Though her thoughts were a million miles away from anything physical, she relished the feel of Emma's hand on her back while the other smoothed her hair. Tender touches that intoxicated her with …

A door slammed shut in the apartment next door and they jolted apart. They stared at each other and then broke into laughter.

'You're gonna be a bigger wreck than me when

this is all over,' Lauren said, guilt already plaguing her for putting Emma on edge.

The laughter faded and they stilled. 'This will be over soon, if I've got anything to do about it.'

Lauren took her hand. 'You'll never know how much those words mean to me.'

'I think I do.'

They looked into each other's eyes, unspoken words passing between them.

Lauren's stomach growled, breaking the moment, and they laughed again.

'Okay, I can take a hint,' Emma said to Lauren's stomach. 'You need feeding and I know just the thing.'

She rose to her feet.

'Where're you going?'

'To Waitrose. I'm going to make you a three-course meal courtesy of Jamie Oliver.'

'Really?'

'Indeed. So go and watch the telly or something, and I'll be back in twenty minutes, max.' She pecked Lauren on the cheek as if it were the most natural thing in the world to do. 'Do you like Banoffee pie?'

'Do I ever! You're not going to attempt to make it, are you?'

'Just watch me,' Emma said and was gone before Lauren could say another word.

Hearing the front door shut, Lauren rose and stood a few feet away from the window, gazing across at her apartment. She wrapped her arms around herself, remembering the warmth of Emma's embrace. Lauren had felt safe in her arms—something she hadn't experienced in a very long time.

Chapter Sixteen

Stalked! The word kept flashing in Emma's mind as she cooked, poured the wine, and served the food. Even while they ate she tried to get her head around it. Mike had driven Lauren away from family and friends—*and me*—without giving anyone a say in the matter. Rage tore at her heart; for fourteen years, Lauren had suffered the loss of a carefree life because some bastard got his kicks from scaring people. If she had known this when she witnessed the burglary, she would have been the first person to run up to Lauren's apartment, taking her chances against the intruder.

She forced down every morsel of food with a mouthful of wine, swallowing around the lump in her throat. Now that she knew the reason for Lauren's disappearance and who was responsible, she wanted to hunt Mike down and throttle him with her bare hands.

Taking Lauren to confront Mike would expose him as the coward he really was—a coward who had tormented her from the shadows. While Emma's emotional turmoil raged within, Lauren rubbed her stomach and leant back in her chair, stretching her feet out beneath the table.

'Oh my word, I feel so guilty.'

'Why?' Emma asked, pushing away her half-eaten plate and picking up her wineglass.

'You prepared a three-course meal and won't even

let me help clean up.'

''Cause you're my guest.'

Lauren gave her a crooked smile. 'I can't remember the last time I was this relaxed. It seems like forever.'

'I'm not surprised. I don't know how I'd cope with having to constantly look over my shoulder. It must have—must be terrifying.' Emma had managed to refrain from talking about Mike for most of the day because she didn't want to sour their time together, but she had to broach the subject. If Lauren were a client, she wouldn't sit around pretending like there wasn't a white elephant in the room.

'It is. Sometimes I feel like going to the Amazon and disappearing forever.'

'Don't you dare. Now that I've found you, I don't want to lose you again.'

Lauren straightened in her seat. 'Emma, you do know I can't stay—in England, that is—whether it turns out to be Mike or not.'

Emma kept her voice level despite the suffocating tightness in her throat. 'Is that because you don't want to, or—'

'I've always wanted to come back,' Lauren cut in. 'More than anything, but my whole life is in Paris.' She gave Emma a sad smile, eyes shining with unexpected tears. 'Besides, even if it is him. It might not change anything. I can't live my life in the shadows, looking over my shoulder, constantly scared of opening the front door …'

Without thinking, Emma slid from her chair and knelt in front of Lauren. 'You won't have to. It's Mike who's harassing you. I know it is. Trust me, after tomorrow, you'll be leading a normal life again.'

Lauren's jaw set. 'I want that more than anything in the world—well, almost anything. It was hard, you know.'

'What was?'

'Leaving you. I mean, I couldn't take them bullying you anymore—that's why I kissed you—only …'

'Go on.'

'Only I wasn't expecting the connection I felt. The intense attraction—it was mad.'

After all these years, I finally know why she kissed me.

A note of tension crept into Emma's voice. 'Why didn't you get in touch, or at least tell me you were going? When you kissed me … it turned my world upside down.'

'Has your life turned upright since?'

'No,' she admitted.

Emma held her breath while Lauren held her gaze; Lauren's grey eyes burrowed into her. Emma licked the curve of her lip, her mouth suddenly dry.

Lauren rose from her chair and pulled Emma to her feet. 'Am I making you uncomfortable?'

'Not at all. I'm not easily shaken.' Her heart was pounding so hard it actually hurt. Heat emanated from Lauren's body, and Emma resisted the urge to fan herself.

'Is that right?' Lauren asked with a slow smile.

'Yes.'

'So I'm wasting my time then?' Lauren said teasingly as she took a small step back.

'Hey, I didn't say that, did I?' The smell of Lauren's perfume intoxicated her. Emma slid her arm around Lauren's waist and drew her near. Thoughts of remaining platonic were banished from her mind. 'I should have added, I'm not easily shaken, most of the time.'

'Are you shaken now?' Lauren asked, gazing at her from under her lashes.

Emma held up her free hand, her eyes dropping to Lauren's chest and the curves of her breasts. 'Trembling.'

Lauren pressed her thigh between Emma's legs. 'Is that because of me?'

Everything below Emma's waist was throbbing and burning as if it had a life of its own. 'All because of you.'

With the tip of her finger, Lauren trailed a line down Emma's neck. 'Do you want to—'

'You read my mind.'

Lauren brushed her lips over Emma's mouth as she said, 'I hope we're on the same page, otherwise I'm in deep trouble if—'

'I'm on page fifty-nine where … where we're interrupted by the bloody bell,' Emma said.

The melodic tune of the doorbell sounded down the hallway. Emma rolled her eyes heavenwards as if some divine intervention could chase the person at the door away so they could carry on with their wonderfully lustful conversation.

'Are you expecting someone?' Uncertainty replaced the desire in Lauren's eyes.

'No,' she murmured, desperate to keep Lauren's attention on her.

The doorbell rang again. Feeling Lauren stiffen in her arms, she released her and walked off to answer the intercom. 'Don't worry. It's probably someone pressing the wrong door number. I'll get rid of them.'

***

Emma stepped back into the kitchen and gestured towards Lauren with a sweep of her arm. 'Surprise. Look who's here.'

Lauren craned her neck to see around Emma. If Lauren was as disappointed as Emma was for the interruption, it didn't show on her face. She looked ecstatic to see a face from her past. Setting aside her own disappointment, Emma was glad to see Lauren happy.

'Hope! Oh my God, it's so good to see you.'

Hope's face remained expressionless, confusion settling in her eyes, and then her mouth curled up. 'Lauren? Lauren! I never thought I'd see you again.'

Lauren feigned disappointment. 'Is that it? No hug?'

'What? Oh, of course. Sorry, I'm just a bit taken aback,' she said, walking towards her.

The women briefly embraced. 'I thought Emma was kidding when she said you were here. How did you two hook up again? It's been, what? Over ten years.'

'Fourteen to be precise,' Emma said, taking a glass from the cupboard and filling it with red wine. She handed it to Hope then refilled Lauren's glass. *Fourteen long, agonising years.*

Maybe I should call my mum and tell her Lauren's returned. Obviously Emma would leave out the part about the stalker and that Lauren would be returning to Paris in the near future, but at least she could show her mother she wasn't a lost cause and that her feelings for Lauren hadn't been a figment of her imagination.

'Where've you been hiding all this time?' Hope asked, sounding critical.

'I haven't been hiding anywhere. I went to Paris to study, that's all.'

Hope snorted. 'Without saying goodbye to anyone?'

'It was complicated, Hope,' Emma broke in irritably.

'Complicated?' Hope repeated as if she hadn't heard her right.

'Lauren, just tell her the truth.' Emma touched Lauren's arm and nodded at the questioning look in her eyes.

Hope watched them suspiciously as she shrugged off her jacket and hung it over the back of the chair. 'What truth?'

Lauren lowered her gaze to her hands. Seconds passed before she spoke. 'Okay, the truth is … I left because someone was stalking me.'

'Stalking you?' Hope laughed. 'No, really, why did

you leave?' Her gaze shifted from her stepsister to Lauren, and seeing that neither of them was playing a prank on her, she asked, 'A stalker? For real? You weren't exactly famous back then. Why would anyone stalk you? No offence, you were magnificently beautiful—you still are, I have to say—but a stalker? That's just bizarre!'

Lauren gave a resigned shrug. 'God knows why. I barely understand it myself.'

'And now the stalker is back,' Emma said matter-of-factly. 'We think it's Mike Foster.'

Mockery invaded Hope's stare. 'Don't be ridiculous. That weedy twerp? How could he possibly know Lauren is in London?'

'It's true. The day I bumped into him, my apartment was burgled. Then yesterday I received a note through my door asking why my lights were still on.'

Hope walked to the window and peered outside. 'Are you saying he could be following you?' She turned back so fast her dark hair swung around her head. 'And you came here, putting Emma in danger?'

'That's a bit dramatic, Hope,' Emma said. 'It's Mike we're talking about.'

'Is it? Is it really? And you know this for sure how?' Hope asked Lauren.

Lauren shook her head. 'I don't have any evidence, if that's what you mean, but—'

'So you don't know. You're basically a sitting duck. A sitting duck hiding out in my sister's apartment.'

'All right, that's enough,' Emma protested, but

Lauren raised a hand to stop her.

'No, Hope's right. I shouldn't be here. I am placing you in danger if Mike isn't responsible. I wasn't thinking straight.'

'You,' Emma said, pointing at Lauren, 'stay right where you are.' She grabbed Hope by the arm. 'And you, come with me!'

Emma marched Hope to the living room and closed the door behind them before starting on her.

'What the hell are you playing at?' Emma hissed, keeping her voice at a level that wouldn't travel to the kitchen.

Hope looked at her incredulously. 'Me? You should be asking her that question.'

'I'm asking you. Why were you so horrible to her?'

Hope's mouth was set in a sullen grimace. 'I'm looking out for you.'

'And I'm looking out for her. She needs my help.'

'Stop playing the bloody saviour for once in your life. She's trouble. I wouldn't put it past her to make this whole thing up to tug on your heartstrings. Oh look, she's already got under your skin again. Isn't it the truth that history repeats itself?'

'Have you quite finished slagging Lauren off.' Emma paused, taking in a deep, steadying breath before speaking again. 'Look, if you can't be civil, I'd prefer it if you left.'

'Leave? Are you joking?' She folded her arms. 'I've been by your side for more than half your life, and you want to toss me aside for her?'

She touched Hope's arm and gently said, 'No, of course not. I'm sorry. I'm just asking for you to show a little compassion.'

'Like she did for you when she left and broke your heart?' Hope wasn't giving an inch.

'You know why—'

'Yeah, Mike the stalker. How could I forget?'

'We're going round in circles here. I want you to play nice. Can you do that? For me?'

Hope rolled her eyes. 'If I have to.'

'Yes, you have to.'

On her way back to the kitchen through the hallway, Emma straightaway noticed the front door was ajar.

'Lauren?' she called out and checked the kitchen. *Empty.* She rushed back to the front door and peeked into the corridor, looking from left to right. Not seeing her, she went back to the living room. 'She's gone! Hope, she left!'

'Good! Let her dump her problems on someone else.' Hope stood in the living room with her arms folded, looking smug.

'Just shut up. For once in your life, know when to shut the fuck up!'

Emma raced out of the apartment and slammed the door behind her in frustration.

She rushed to the stairwell and looked down. Nothing. Pressing the lift button, Emma tapped her foot. *Please don't let her have heard what Hope said.*

***

The lift door opened and Emma rushed out into the darkness, shoving her arms into her jacket as she checked the street for any sign of Lauren. Her mind was so focused on Lauren and her safety that she didn't hear the stranger come up behind her.

'Hey!' a voice said.

Shocked by the unexpected presence, Emma's hand flew to her mouth to stifle a scream. *Is it Mike? Did he follow Lauren to my building?* The harder she tried to calm her mind, the more frantic it became.

As she tensed, ready to turn, the man spoke again. 'Ms Clary? Don't be scared. I just want to talk. Honest.'

How does he know my name? She frowned. Whoever it was, he didn't sound threatening, nor did he sound like a grown man. More like a very well-spoken, educated young boy whose voice had recently broken. Reassured that whoever was behind her meant no harm, she turned to face him.

A small gasp escaped her lips. The person standing in front of her couldn't have been much older than eighteen. He was tall and painfully thin, but it was his face—in particular, the large swollen eye—that drew her attention. It looked like the man had gone one round in the boxing ring with Mike Tyson. The rest of his face wasn't any better: swollen red lumps, a split lip, one very black eye, bruised cheeks. Whoever had done this to him had wanted to go beyond hurting him. She'd go as far as to say that death had been on his attacker's mind.

'How do you know my name?' she asked, unable to take her gaze away from his eye. She'd never seen anything like it in real life. The stretched skin, painted deep purple with bruising that looked black in places, shone. His eye was almost swollen shut. He must have been in agony from it, let alone from the other cuts and bruises.

'I'm sorry to bother you like this …'

Emma narrowed her eyes and leant forward to get a better look at him. Her senses were detecting something, but she couldn't quite put her finger on it.

'I followed you from work yesterday to find out where you live. I was too scared to approach you then. Anyway, I woke up this morning with a bit more courage so I've been hanging around today on the off chance you'd go to the shops.'

'Why? Why would you do that?' she asked angrily.

'Because I need to speak to you.'

'About what?'

'About Louise.'

Aha! That was it. Something else clicked, and Emma peered closer at the young man in the dim light of the streetlamp. He wasn't a he, but a she, though it was very easy to mistake her for a man with her close-cropped hair and puffy jacket. *Did she assault Louise?*

'How do you know Louise?' she asked.

'I'm her friend, Jay. I know what you must have heard about me, but it's not true—'

'Are you fucking kidding me? You assaulted an innocent young girl and you followed me home.'

'Please, look, Ms Clary, please look at my phone.' Jay thrust her phone into Emma's face. It showed Louise with her arms around Jay's neck, kissing her lips. 'This picture was taken just before her dad came in and caught us.'

'Showing me a picture doesn't mean you didn't assault her.' Emma hurried across the road, still scanning the area for any sign of Lauren. 'Seriously, you need to back off before I call the police and get you charged with harassment.'

Jay followed her, fiddling with her phone. 'Okay, okay. Please, just read this and I swear I'll go. Please. Look at the date.'

Emma couldn't tell whether her pained expression was because of her injuries or the memory of the beating she'd taken. Reluctantly, she stopped walking and took the phone. She read the WhatsApp messages between Louise and Jay, dated the previous evening. The last few messages were telling:

> Louise: *sorry for what my dad did. R u ok?*
> Jay: *yeah. Worried bout you tho*
> Louise: *Don't, i love you*
> Jay: *love you too babe*

'I take it Louise's father did that to your face,' Emma said, giving her the benefit of the doubt and handing back her phone. She noted that Louise been offline since Jay's last message and could only assume that her parents had taken her phone away.

Emma started walking towards Lauren's building, Jay close behind her.

Jay snorted. 'That's nothing compared to the rest of my body.'

'Look, just tell me what you want. I have to be somewhere.'

'Thank you for believing me.'

'I didn't say anything about believing you. Until I hear it from Louise's mouth, I'm still undecided.'

'Fair enough. But that's what I want. I want you to speak with Louise and tell her she can date whoever she wants. That it's not up to her parents.'

'Was Louise's dad aware you were a girl when he beat the crap out of you?'

Jay stopped and caught Emma's wrist, turning her around. 'I'm not a girl. I may have a female body, but that's as far as it goes.'

'I'm sorry, Jay. My mistake.' She looked up at him.

'The hormones haven't kicked in yet.'

Emma decided to leave that one alone; now definitely was not the time to get into a discussion about transgender issues, and it was none of her business anyway.

The pleading expression on Jay's bruised face weakened her defences. 'Look, I would help but you're out of luck, I'm afraid. I'm the last person her family wants anywhere near her—after you, that is.'

Jay touched his eye tenderly and Emma's heart went out to him. He was just a kid. What could she possibly do to help him?

'Jay, the situation I'm in means that if I contact her, I'll lose my job. Believe me, I'm as worried about her as you are.' Emma closed her eyes, the heaviness of her life weighing on her shoulders.

Jay pushed his cut hands into his jacket pockets. 'I don't think she's safe in that house. Her dad's crazy, and I don't mean that in a rude way. You just have to look at what he did to me.'

Louise's father had certainly crossed the line. To be fair, she didn't know what she would do if she ever walked in on her daughter and thought a boy was attacking her. As far as Louise's parents were concerned, she was a lesbian. They would have been shocked to find their daughter with who they thought was a man.

'You think I deserved it, don't you?' Jay asked.

'Never! I don't believe in violence of any sort,' she said truthfully and racked her brain for something she could do to help. Her options were limited.

'The only thing I can do is have a word with my boss,' Emma said, coming to a stop outside Lauren's building. 'But I'm telling you now: if I find out you've lied to me—'

'I swear I haven't. Just ask Louise. She'll tell you the truth.'

'Give me your number. I'll call you and let you know what's going on, okay? That's the best I can do.'

'Thank you,' Jay said. He called out his number, and Emma tapped it into her phone. 'You're a lifesaver.'

'So I've been told. Will you be all right?' Emma asked, jerking her head towards his face.

Jay prodded his eye and winced. 'Yeah, but I'll be even better if you get back to me with good news.'

'Now go home'—Emma glanced up at Lauren's building—'and keep out of trouble.'

'I will. Thanks for taking the time to listen.' Jay thanked her again and walked into the dark of the night.

Braithwaite House stood tall in front of her as Emma stepped up to the intercom. She buzzed once. No answer. Twice. Nothing. Willing herself to remain calm, she buzzed again.

A tinny voice answered, 'Hello?'

'Lauren? It's Emma. Can I come up?'

'Not right now.'

Lauren must have heard what Hope said and was understandably upset.

'Please. I'm sorry about Hope. If you don't let me in, I'll start begging. Do you want strangers to see me begging in the street? Leave me a bit of dignity, won't you?'

Laughter crackled through the intercom, and then the door buzzed open.

Minutes later, Emma stepped out on Lauren's floor and her stomach did somersaults. They'd been so close to sharing an intimate moment before Hope's arrival. Maybe fate was doing them a favour. What was the point in starting something before they solved Lauren's stalking problem?

Lauren's door was ajar, which Emma took as an invitation for her to walk straight in. As soon as she stepped into the hallway, she heard an unfamiliar, fraught female voice with a thick French accent. Confused, she stopped in her tracks. Her first thought was to call out to Lauren, but she decided against it and confidently strode into the living room. Lauren was sitting on the sofa, and a short-haired woman stood over her, hands on her hips. The stern looks on their faces made it obvious they'd been arguing. *Why though? And who is this woman?*

'Am I interrupting something?' Emma asked, more confused than ever.

'Yes,' the dark-haired woman said without taking her eyes off Lauren.

'No,' Lauren said, looking up at Emma.

'It all makes sense,' the dark-haired woman said sarcastically. 'Is this your new protector?' She gestured towards Emma.

Lauren shook her head. 'Cut it out, Fiona.'

'What else am I supposed to think?' Fiona asked.

'Nothing. That's what. This has nothing to do with you. You are not part of my life anymore, and I want you to leave.'

'I'm not going anywhere. Not until you—'

'I think you're unsettling her—Fiona, is it?' Emma said upon seeing Lauren's distraught face. 'I think it's best you do as she asks.'

'You do, huh?'

'Yes.'

'And what the fuck are you going to do if I don't?' Fiona glared at Emma, dark eyes flashing venomously.

'Call the police.'

'And what do you think they'll do? Arrest me? For what? Protecting my girlfriend?' She laughed at the surprised look on Emma's face. 'Idiote!'

Lauren stood. 'Stop, Fiona! This has gone on long enough. You are not my girlfriend. You are my ex-girlfriend! And don't you dare speak to Emma like that.'

'Emma?' Fiona appraised her. 'Hmm … Emma? Where have I heard that name before?' She clicked her fingers. 'Ahh! I remember! 'er first school-girl crush. So the star-crossed lovers meet again. If it wasn't so pathetic, it would be sweet. Perhaps you two can sell your story to Disney.'

Lauren walked towards the front door and held it open. 'Get out of here, Fiona, and I swear if you come back, I'll call the police myself.'

'Is that a fact?'

'Yes.'

'I 'ave a feeling I'll be seeing you again soon when you realise *she* doesn't 'ave what it takes to look after you.'

'I'll take my chances. Please go.' Lauren pointed at the open door. 'Now!'

'Whatever.' Fiona glared at Emma as she passed.

As soon as Fiona left, Lauren walked back into the living room and collapsed on the sofa.

'Jesus!' Emma said, running her hand through her hair and shaking her head in amazement. 'If I wasn't so sure it was Mike stalking you, she'd be my primary suspect. She's one scary lady.'

'It's all a front,' Lauren said. 'She's really not that

bad when she's not acting all territorial.'

'Somehow, I find that hard to believe.' Emma sat next to her on the sofa. 'What was she doing here?'

'She wants to get back together.'

'Oh okay.' Emma fiddled with the zip on her coat, unsure of what to say but with a multitude of questions begging to be asked.

'I'm not getting back with her, don't worry about that. I wouldn't have normally let her in but when I got back to the apartment block she was waiting outside. For a few minutes I stupidly felt sorry for her. I should have known.'

'What was she giving you a hard time about?'

'This.' Lauren passed her the paper scrunched in her hand. 'I found it when I got home. It wasn't hand delivered this time. There's a postage stamp on it.'

Emma gently unfolded it and stared at the text long and hard. The page had a short message on it: **I'm coming for you, Lauren. Soon.**

No wonder her ex is vexed. Shit!

'Well that's something at least?' Emma said, looking over the envelope. 'Mike knows he can't get back in the building.'

Lauren shrugged. 'Fiona thinks he's mentally ill.'

The thought unsettled her. 'Let's not give people with mental health problems a bad name. He doesn't have a chemical imbalance. He's just a sicko who gets cheap thrills out of scaring people.'

'It's working.'

'Only until tomorrow. Look, Lauren, about what

Hope said—'

'It's okay. I wasn't offended. She was just saying what she felt but at the same time I didn't feel comfortable staying while you had that discussion.'

'You know I don't agree with her.'

'I know.'

'Good. I'm glad that's settled. Now, do you want me to stay on the sofa tonight?'

'Would you mind? I don't wanna be alone.'

Emma took hold of Lauren's hand, the softness of her skin sending her back to the intimate moment they shared earlier. 'Of course not. Go and have a hot bath. I'll guard the fort,' she said and leant over to kiss her on the cheek.

Lauren turned and their lips met in a brief kiss.

'My brave hero,' Lauren whispered, stroking the side of Emma's face with her hand.

A smile played on Emma's lips. 'You know heroes normally get more than one kiss in the movies.'

'Are we in the movies?'

Inching her face forward, Emma said, 'If we use our imagination we can be where ever we want to be.'

Their lips met again and all the years of heartbreak and unfulfillment dissipated. They were together again, yet a barrier still obstructed their path.

Emma pulled away from the kiss and slumped back on the sofa.

'What's wrong?' Lauren asked, disappointment evident in her grey eyes.

Emma stared up unblinkingly into the air.

'Nothing's wrong. I just don't think you're in the right frame of mind at the moment to take things further. I feel like I'm taking advantage.'

Lauren grinned. 'Don't be silly. I know *exactly* what I'm doing.'

'Even so … Go on, go and get in the bath,' she said giving Lauren's knee a rub.

Emma watched Lauren in silence until she disappeared from the room. All the while wishing she could rewind time to just a few minutes ago. She wanted desperately to feel Lauren writhe and surge beneath her. To taste her sweetness. To …

She fought to keep her horniness under control. Emma wanted Lauren more than anything but the circumstances had to be right. If she slept with Lauren and Lauren left, Emma doubted her heart would ever recover.

Why can't I be strong enough to just go with the flow?

Until the situation with Mike was sorted it would have to remain a fantasy.

Damn you, Mike Foster!

Chapter Seventeen

Lauren let out a long yawn and stretched her legs. She hadn't slept straight through the night in ages. *All because of beautiful, sweet Emma.*

She had enjoyed her rallying speech; it had encouraged Lauren to take up the sword and go to battle with an invisible enemy. Reaching over to her bedside table, she scooped up her mobile phone and switched it on. The first thing she noted when it came to life was that it was 9:00 a.m. The second thing was several messages from Frankie. Worried something was wrong, she called him.

'Frankie, is everything okay?'

'Your phone was off,' he snapped.

'Sorry, had a stress—'

'I couldn't get hold of you, Lauren, I told you before about this.'

She pushed herself into a sitting position. 'I said I'm sorry.'

'I was worried. I thought something had happened to you.'

'I'm fine.' Her tone softened. The stress from her life seemed to be filtering into the people closest to her.

'I came round. Why didn't you answer your door?'

'I turned the ringer off, I just wanted a peaceful evening with Emma and no disturbances,' she said.

'Emma? Did she stay the night?'

Lauren could hear the disapproval in his voice and it immediately got her back up. Lately, Frankie had got in the habit of interfering with her life, something he hadn't done in all the years she'd known him. If anything, Frankie was one of the most laid back people she'd ever met.

'Not that it's any of your business, but yes, she did. I got another letter.'

'What did it say this time?'

She relayed the message to him, and his voice was forceful when he said, 'That's it, you're coming to stay with me, and I won't take no for an answer.'

'I'm afraid you'll have to, because I'm not leaving here—'

'I'm starting to think you're taking this matter too lightly.' He gave a bitter laugh. 'You've had a break-in and two threatening letters and you're telling me you want to stay there?'

'If you'd let me finish. I think I know who the stalker is.'

'What! Who? How did you find out?'

'It's a long story. Can we meet up for lunch and I'll tell you all about it? I've got a busy morning ahead.'

'All right. I won't say another word about it until I hear your side of things.'

'I'll see you at midday?'

'Yes sure. There's a place called Gavan's near the South Bank. I think you'll like it there.'

'Sounds great, I'll Google the address. See you then.'

The line fell silent. It felt strange having so many people pull her in different directions. At home, alone in Paris, life was simpler. She had her daily routine and no interference. Not even her parents hassled her when they visited. In the last few days, it was as though she had become a child again. Pushing all thoughts of Frankie aside, she swung her legs over the side of the bed and went in search of Emma.

'Something smells good,' Lauren said, tracking her to the kitchen, where she was making breakfast. She walked over to the hob and peeked at the frying pan sizzling with several slices of bacon. *Bacon butty, my favourite.*

'Good morning. Did you sleep well?' Emma asked, coming up behind her and handing her a mug of coffee.

Lauren felt guilty admitting the truth—she had slept well—because Emma looked tired and apprehensive. 'Like a newborn baby on her mother's bosom.'

'Okay, if that works for you. So what's on your agenda today?'

'I've decided to go to the police.'

'You have? That's great!'

'And then I'm going to see Mike—alone.' Lauren held her hand up to silence Emma's protests. 'This is something I have to do for my own peace of mind.'

'But—'

Irritation trickled in as it normally did when someone tried to tell her what was best for her. 'There are no buts. I'm going to his workplace. What's he going to do in broad daylight in front of a load of shoppers?'

'You seem pretty calm about all this.'

'I am now that I know who my stalker is. Mike isn't a threat to me. There's no reason to think he's capable of anything beyond threatening me from a distance.'

'Do you fancy meeting up later?'

'Can we leave it until tomorrow? I'm going to see Frankie. I don't know how long I'll be.'

Emma turned the gas off and removed the bacon from the pan with a fork, placing them between buttered slices of white bread. She handed a plate to Lauren. 'Oh, okay. Give me a call when you're ready.'

'Please don't spend the day worrying about me,' Lauren said taking a bite of her sandwich. 'Everything will be fine.'

She hoped she sounded more convincing than she felt.

***

Lauren stood patiently in line, waiting behind an irate man moaning about the long queue. They had been queuing for over forty-five minutes while a bored-looking policeman with blond curls took details from a woman complaining about kids creating havoc in her neighbourhood. He showed as much interest in her story as he would watching paint dry. He would no doubt show her the same courtesy when it was her turn, but she didn't care. Not anymore. She was after one thing from the officer; after that, knock on wood, she would never have to see the inside of a police station again.

Another half hour passed before Lauren reached the police officer.

'How can I help?' he asked, barely glancing at her.

'Someone I used to go to school with is stalking me.'

'Has he threatened you?'

'Yes.' She withdrew the notes from her pocket. 'He sent me these. I think he's the same person who's been stalking me since I was at school.'

'You think?'

'Yes, I think.' She gave him a summarised version of events that dated back to her school days, then she explained the coincidence of the letters arriving after she'd bumped into Mike following her return to London after a fourteen-year absence.

The officer nodded, and to Lauren's surprise, he seemed to buy her theory wholesale.

'What information do you have on this person?'

'Well, I know that he works at Tesco in Lewisham.'

The officer wrote down the information, along with Mike's name. He then gave her a crime number and contact details. This was the dynamite Lauren needed to show Mike she wasn't messing around. She clutched onto the paper as if her life depended on it.

'Someone will have a chat with this chap. In the meantime, if he bothers you again, contact us using these details.'

'When will an officer go to see him?'

'Shortly,' he said.

It was clear he didn't want to lock himself into a timeframe. Her complaint was probably the least of his worries when there were far more serious cases to deal with.

'Okay, thank you.'

Stepping outside into the bright sunshine, she exhaled a deep breath. That wasn't as bad as she'd thought. She actually felt quite positive about the encounter. Emma was right. Things had changed. *One down, one to go.*

Lauren took a cab to Mike's workplace, not because she was fearful of being exposed on the street, but because she wanted to get the confrontation over with as fast as possible. She didn't even know whether he was at work that day, but it didn't bother her. If he wasn't, she would return every day until she finally spoke to him.

Tesco in Lewisham was a superstore, and there were plenty of people milling about. If there was one saving grace for bumping into Mike the previous week, it was that she knew what he looked like. Since she'd last seen him all those years ago, he could have completely changed his appearance.

Unfortunately, after walking aimlessly around the car park and inside the store, Lauren hadn't found Mike anywhere.

And this is why I'd make a crap detective. Disheartened, she considered asking for his whereabouts at the customer service desk, but she didn't want to lose the element of surprise. When she finally told him about the letters and what the consequences had been on her life, she wanted to see an organic reaction from him, not a prepared one.

Lauren glanced at the time on her phone. *Damn.* She would have to come back tomorrow. It was nearly midday and she was late for her meeting with Frankie.

***

Lauren entered Gavan's thirty minutes late. It was a small intimate restaurant with wooden beams dominating the ceiling, and chunky oak furniture giving the place a rustic feel. Being only a few minutes' walk from the South Bank, the restaurant was already crowded with diners. Lauren spotted Frankie as soon as she entered, luckily he had managed to secure them a table by the window. As Lauren wandered over to him she imagined how romantic the setting would look in evening, with candles on the tables and soft music playing in the background. She made a mental note to return with Emma.

He stood when he saw her.

'I'm so sorry I'm late,' she said, pecking him on the cheek.

'Don't worry, I only got here ten minutes ago myself. I hope you don't mind, but I ordered the seafood platter to share,' he said, sitting down.

'That's fine,' she replied, draping her coat over the back of the chair before sliding onto her seat.

Frankie looked at her expectantly. 'Right, now tell

me what the hell is going on.'

A waiter stopped by the table and Lauren ordered a latte.

When they were alone, she said to Frankie, 'I finally know who my stalker is.'

'Who?'

'Do you remember when I told you I bumped into someone I went to school with?'

'It isn't him!'

'Yes. Emma convinced me. It all makes sense now. Anyway, I've reported him to the police.'

'I thought they were useless?'

'They were years ago. Seems they take harassment more seriously these days. They're gonna have a word with him. I can't believe this nightmare is nearly over.'

He squeezed her hand. 'I hope so, you deserve a break from all the stress.'

'Just to think if you hadn't persuaded me to come back, I would still be running.'

The intensity in Frankie's eyes lessened to something calmer. 'After all this time, you can finally reclaim your life.'

And the woman I left behind.

Chapter Eighteen

Emma's intention was to go home and have a lazy Sunday. *Was* being the operative word. Instead she found herself jumping on a bus heading towards Kennington. Since Jay's unexpected visit, Louise had been on her mind. Emma had to make sure she was okay and confirm Jay's story, regardless of the wrath she would face from Gina.

Louise lived in a quiet crescent with oak trees hugging the curved street. The day was pleasant enough, with the sun peeking out from behind white clouds and birds twittering from the bare tree branches. It was lucky Emma had a good memory. Considering all the forms she filled in each day, she was still able to remember Louise's address.

Number 57 was a terraced redbrick building, with a neat compact garden that had a double-tier waterfall in the centre. Emma found the sound of the water soothing as she rang the bell and stood waiting. She would have been lying if she'd said she wasn't nervous. This time tomorrow, she might be dragging Lauren with her to the job centre.

Emma did her best not to think about how things were going with Lauren.

Footsteps approached the door and she braced herself.

The door opened and Louise's face paled at the

sight of her. 'Ms Clary? What … what are you doing here?'

'We need to talk.'

Louise glanced behind her. 'You shouldn't have come. I'll get into trouble.'

'More trouble than your friend Jay?'

Louise gasped. 'Jay? How did you …?'

'He came to see me.'

'He did what? That idiot. I knew I shouldn't have told him anything about you.'

'I need to know the truth, Louise, what happened with Jay? Did he attack you?'

'Of course he didn't, he's my boyfriend. My dad has just blown this out of proportion.'

'Who you talking to, Lou?' a male voice asked from inside the house.

Louise looked uncertain how to answer. 'Um … it's no one.'

'You're talking to someone.' The voice grew nearer, and then its owner appeared behind Louise.

Emma did a double take. Instead of the big macho man she had envisaged, Mr Willis couldn't have been taller than five foot three. His build was slight and his left eye had a twitch. She couldn't believe the man standing in front of her was responsible for the damage inflicted on Jay.

'Mr Willis, I'm—'

'I know who you are. What do you want?' he asked in a soft-spoken voice.

'To talk.'

'We've got nothing to say to you, Ms Clary. I thought I made that clear to your boss.'

He started to close the door, but Emma pushed it back. 'I'm sorry, Louise, but I have to tell your father the truth.'

'The truth about what?' Mr Willis asked.

She hesitated, desperately thinking of a suitable way to explain the situation. 'The young man you assaulted—'

'So you're one of those appeaser types. What would you have done, Ms Clary, if you'd come home and found a thug raping your child? Invite them to join you for dinner once it was over?'

He looked at her with disgust, revealing the rage bottled up inside.

Emma turned her attention to Louise. 'Please, you need to tell your dad what happened.'

'I saw what happened with my own eyes. Now get off my property. I have never hit a woman before, but right this minute, I'm sorely tempted.'

'What's it to be, Louise?' Emma asked, backing away.

'I'm sorry. I can't,' Louise mouthed. The expression on her face was one of regret as her dad pulled her inside and slammed the door shut.

Emma let out a pent-up breath and started down the path. *That didn't go too well now did it, Ms Busy Body?*

Standing at the bottom of the path, she looked back in time to see the curtain flutter at the window on the ground floor. All she could do was hope that her words sank into Louise's subconscious and persuaded her to do the right thing.

Emma took out her mobile to call Lauren. Realising only a few hours had passed since they parted ways, she stuffed her phone back into her pocket. She didn't want to seem too eager. Besides, waiting a whole day to see her again meant she could get on with the house work she'd been putting off. *Or I can spend the night wrapped up in the quilt Lauren slept in.* She didn't have to think twice about how she'd be spending her evening.

Chapter Nineteen

The early morning sky was shrouded in slate grey clouds as Lauren hailed a taxi and made her way to Waterloo. Her first stop of the day was Enterprise car hire. If she were going to stake out Tesco for an extended period of time, hiring a car was the best option. The school run meant traffic along Lambeth Palace Road was horrendous. Cars were jammed together, barely leaving an inch of space, but the taxi driver didn't seem too bothered. After all, the meter was running. Still, it was a mild relief to be held up. The delay offered her a reprieve from the anxiety that had hounded her since leaving her apartment.

She stared out of the window as the taxi inched along, past Lambeth Palace and St Thomas' Hospital. Why did her courage disappear as soon as she was away from Emma? By not seeing her last night, not only had she missed her terribly, but her confidence had wilted. Perhaps it was because she took after her mother, who constantly looked to her dad as the strong one, the 'rescuer', the person who would make everything right in her world. *Maybe that's what I'm doing with Emma. Turning her into my rescuer.*

Eventually the traffic became unglued and cars broke free, moving forward at a faster pace. Ahead, she could make out the distinctive green logo of the car hire shop. Lauren rummaged inside her bag for her purse and double-checked she had her driving licence. She didn't want to have to make the same trip twice in one day. Once the driver pulled up outside the building, she slipped him a twenty pound note through the small gap in the partition to cover the fare.

Inside the sleek office, the space felt dark and gloomy despite the white walls and floor to ceiling windows, as if the weather outside had managed to cast its shadow inside the building. Lauren took her place behind a couple of customers waiting to be served by the tall, lanky salesman behind the raised counter. He wore a dark grey suit and a crisp white shirt. Lauren watched him as he swiftly dealt with each customer in a happy, confident manner.

When Lauren stepped up to be served, his reception was no different, and she told him her requirements. She squinted to make out his name tag: Nick.

'How long do you want to hire the car for?' Nick asked. He looked up at her from the computer screen.

'Three days,' she said, thinking that would be enough time to catch Mike. She could always get an extension if needed.

'Visiting family?' he asked in a conversational tone as he typed in the details from her driving licence.

'Um, no. Just need a run-around for a few days.'

'Cool,' he said cheerfully. He printed the paperwork and slid it across the counter towards her with a pen.

After photocopying her driving licence and taking

payment, Nick led the way to her hire car: a black 2015 Ford Fiesta with black fabric seats. The interior wasn't overly spacious, but it suited her purposes. It wasn't as if she was going on a long-distance trip. The furthest she would be driving was three miles away.

Buckling her seatbelt, she rearranged the rear-view mirror so she had a clear view behind her and started the engine. It purred like a kitten. Shifting into reverse, she slowly edged her way out of the hire car's garage and headed towards Lewisham.

Grateful for the built-in satellite navigation system and its ability to plot a faster route, Lauren realised it would have taken her an age to get to Lewisham without using the back streets. London had changed so much since her last visit. Every inch of the city seemed to be cluttered with fashionable, unpronounceable restaurants or luxury apartments. Even the layout seemed alien to her. Roads had been widened and the amount of traffic seemed worse than she remembered. *And I thought driving in Paris was manic.*

The journey didn't take too long, and she was soon turning off a small roundabout and following a sign towards Tesco. She queued behind a line of cars waiting to get into the car park.

When the traffic dispersed, she crawled along, searching for a space. She needed to get as close to the entrance as possible to spot Mike when he entered or left the building. Luckily, as she neared the entrance, a van pulled out and she manoeuvred the small car backwards into the spot with ease. Switching the engine off, she unbuckled her seatbelt, leant forward, and stared through the car window at the main entrance. Seeing a flurry of young, attractive women, she wondered whether Mike had stalked any of them. If he had the inclination to stalk one person, he might have made a habit of it. Maybe someone else had reported him to the police, which would only add weight to her complaint.

Lauren glanced at the digital clock on the dashboard. Whether Mike would show up today was anyone's guess, but it was a gamble she was willing to take. She preferred sitting there, where she felt in control, rather than at home, waiting for the flap on her letterbox to open.

It's a pity I didn't think to bring a flask of coffee with me. If he didn't make an appearance that day she'd make sure she brought enough to keep her going next time. Lauren had thought about borrowing Emma's binoculars, until she realised how peculiar she would look spying on shoppers. Management would no doubt call the police if they caught her.

She turned on the radio for company and settled back in her seat, not daring to take her eyes off the entrance, not even when her phone rang hours later. Feeling around for it in her bag, she accepted the call.

'Hello.'

'Hello, Lone Ranger.'

Lauren's lips curved at the sound of Emma's voice. 'Hello yourself.'

'Where're you now?'

'At Tesco.' Lauren kneaded the tense muscles behind her neck. 'I'm still in the car park, waiting to see if Mike turns up.'

'Are you kidding? How long have you been there?'

'Hours.' Lauren had committed herself to confronting Mike, and she wouldn't leave until she achieved her goal. If she had to hang around until midnight, so be it.

'Fancy some company? I can bring a quilt to snuggle under.'

As much as Lauren wanted Emma by her side, she didn't want to take advantage of her generosity or her time.

'Ha! We'd probably get mistaken for homeless people and be moved on. Besides, I'm warm enough. I hired a car.'

'I've always dreamt of doing something like that: staking someone out in a car. We can be like Cagney and Lacey.'

'At least Cagney and Lacey got paid for their time.' Noting the raindrops on the windscreen, Lauren turned the ignition and flipped on the wipers to clear her view.

'I'm a sucker to be taken advantage of. What do you say? Can I join you? I'll bring coffee and snacks.'

Lauren should have said no, but she was a little parched. *A caffeine jolt is just what I need.* Anyway, two sets of eyes were better than one. 'Okay, you've twisted my arm.'

'I hope that's not the only reason you want me to come,' Emma said.

Lauren stifled the instinct to tell her the truth: that if it were possible, she would spend every minute of every day with her. Instead, she said, 'Coffee and good company. Who could say no to that?'

'I'd say I have more to offer than that, but pointing out my positive attributes can wait. I'll be there ASAP. What car are you driving?'

'A black Ford Fiesta. I'm opposite the entrance.'

'Be there before you know it.'

The line went dead, and Lauren threw the phone onto the passenger seat. Resting her chin on the steering wheel, she said, 'Come on, Mike, where are you? Show yourself.'

She imagined the other things—positive, constructive things—she could be doing with her time. Not only to do with work, but with Emma as well. How strange that the very situation that had torn them apart years ago was now the glue holding them together. Because of Emma, Lauren had found the strength to face her stalker. Any other time she would have hightailed it back to Paris without another thought.

Thinking about Emma, Lauren almost called her back and begged her to hurry. A day away from her had been too long.

Half an hour passed, and a knock on the passenger side window startled her. She snapped her head around and looked straight into Emma's apologetic eyes. Emma was wearing the same red leather jacket as when she had shown up unexpectedly at her apartment. Lauren liked the way it hugged her figure, the V-neck finish exposing a small area of her bare chest. She had to mentally kick herself to stop from thinking about what lay beneath it. Instead, she thought about how much she liked Emma's hair when her ponytail was a loose plait slung over her left shoulder. *A much safer vision to focus on.*

'Are you gonna let me in?' Emma asked with a laugh.

Quickly removing her phone and bag from the front seat and throwing it in the back, Lauren pressed the automatic switch that unlocked the doors.

'Sorry, I didn't mean to scare you,' Emma said, handing Lauren two hot coffees in a cardboard holder and a sandwich before slipping into the seat beside her.

Lauren handed Emma her coffee and took the lid off her cup. The rich aroma of coffee beans filled the small space. 'Don't worry. I was miles away.'

'Thinking about something good, I hope.' Emma set her coffee cup on the dashboard and shrugged off her jacket.

'You could say that,' Lauren said her eyes focused ahead.

'Still a no-show?'

Lauren bit her lip and shook her head.

Digging into her shoulder bag, Emma took out her iPad. 'First, let me say I'm a hundred percent convinced Mike's your stalker, but I thought there wouldn't be any harm if we widened the circle to make sure we haven't overlooked anyone. I mean there is a tiny, tiny possibility it could be someone different to your original stalker. Maybe even a copycat, someone who knows what happened to you and are playing on your fears.'

'I'd have to be pretty unlucky don't you think?' Lauren said.

'Stranger things have happened. I've been researching stalkers online and found this questionnaire on a website called "Who's Stalking You". You in the mood to answer a few questions?'

Lauren opened her sandwich. It wasn't until she took her first bite that she realised how hungry she was. She nodded, encouraging Emma to carry on as she kept her eyes glued on Tesco's entrance.

'Here goes,' Emma said, launching straight in with her first question without taking a breath. 'Most victims are stalked by someone they know. Can you think of anyone apart from Mike, in this case, who has shown excessive interest in you?'

Lauren gave it some thought, feeling Emma's gaze on her. It was strange, sitting in a cramped space in a supermarket car park reliving her past. Maybe she really had missed something. If so she owed it to herself to look at every detail, no matter how unrelated it might seem. Besides, coming up with ideas on how to find the person responsible for making her life a living hell seemed to make Emma happy. In that sense, answering a few questions was definitely worth it.

'No, not really. I generally keep to myself.'

The shock of realising that isolation was another price she had paid due to fear saddened her. Bar Frankie, she didn't have any real friends, no one she was really close to. Even after living in Paris all those years,

Fiona was the only person she had really opened up to. Of course being a street photographer meant she talked to strangers daily but there was never any meaningful connection. Taking photos from afar and then asking permission to use the image sometimes perturbed people. As if their privacy had been invaded. Why did she choose that career? *Because it gave me control back.* In a sense she had become a stalker herself; capturing people going about their lives, in some instances photographing them when they were at their most vulnerable.

Emma shifted in her seat. 'Is there an ex-partner in your life who doesn't want to let go?'

That was easy. Fiona had been her only real partner. Yes, she'd had brief flings with other people but never anything serious.

'Only Fiona, but I ended things with her over seven months ago. She only knows where I'm staying because my mum told her plus the burglary happened before she arrived. To be honest, I haven't really done any serious dating, before or after.'

Lauren still couldn't understand why she'd lowered her guard with Fiona, letting her into her life. *Loneliness. I've got even more of it to look forward to once I leave London … and Emma.*

Emma looked upwards, tabulating the information. 'What about Fiona's ex-partners? Are any of them on the scene? Could they be jealous of you?'

'Nope. Not that I know of anyway.'

Lauren stared at Emma, contemplating a future without her. Could she really do it? Leave her again?

What was her life worth merely existing in Paris? She'd felt alive since reuniting with Emma. Energy coursed through her veins and she couldn't wait for dawn to break just to see her again.

'She's a very attractive woman,' Emma said, eyes focused on the screen in her hands.

Lauren turned away. 'Fiona? Yes, she is.'

'How did you meet?'

The sky split open, releasing a torrent of rain that viciously battered the top of the car. Neither woman seemed to notice. Lauren could sense Emma's eagerness to learn about her ex, and Lauren couldn't believe that the woman she thought she had been in love with was only a blip in her memory. Sitting there with her, Lauren felt like Emma was the only woman who had ever owned her heart. *The only one who could ever win it.*

'Fiona's an artist,' Lauren started, her eyes momentarily following people with bags overflowing with food as they dashed for cover from the downpour. 'She was showing her work at a gallery I attended. I was impressed with her passion for her art. She said she'd never paint again unless I had dinner with her.'

Emma rolled her eyes. 'I'll have to use that line sometime—not.'

'And the rest is history, as they say.' Had she known how things would turn out, she would have happily let Fiona retire.

Emma closed the cover over her iPad and put it back into her bag. 'If only the police could take the fingerprints from the letters and match them to Mike's.'

'Yeah, like that'll happen. He'd have to be pretty stupid to send them with his fingerprints all over them.'

'You never know.'

Lauren pressed her fingers to her temples. 'So after that questionnaire, we're back to square one.'

'Yeah—Hey, hold on a minute!' Emma's excitement broke through the darkness. 'We don't have to wait for him to turn up here.'

'We don't?'

'No. You know that saying about Google being your friend? Well, so is Facebook. It's a long shot but there's a function called "Friendship Map" which allows you to see your friends' location.'

'Are you serious?' The thought of people willingly giving up private information without a second thought of what it could lead to appalled her. That was one of the reasons she didn't have any social media accounts and why the phone she used was a cheap Nokia; its only function was to make and receive calls. Technology had gone too far in the way of allowing strangers to know your every move.

'Very serious. I'll add him as a friend, I'm sure he'll remember me. If he accepts we should be able to see exactly where he is. We'll even know his address.'

'I don't want to go to his house. It has to be somewhere public.'

'Okay, don't worry we'll concentrate on his workplace then.'

'What if he doesn't accept your friend request?'

'Then we stick to the good old-fashioned stakeout.'

Lauren liked it when Emma said 'we'. It felt good to have someone fighting beside her.

'Do you fancy a bodyguard for the night?' Emma ventured.

'Depends.' Heat rose inside her, bringing her perilously close to saying something she might very well regret in the morning.

'On?'

Lauren looked her over with raised eyebrows. 'On whether she's five foot eight and has smouldering brown eyes …'

Amusement danced in Emma's eyes. 'I think I can conjure up someone like that.'

Lauren liked Emma's flirtatious nature—*a lot.*

'That's sorted then. I'll get a takeaway on the way.' Lauren put the car into drive and headed home. Having Emma nearby was reassuring, but it was also very tempting.

***

'Just water for me, thanks.'

'No wine?' Emma asked, her face emerging from the side of the fridge door.

'Nah.' Lauren unpacked the Chinese silver containers and spooned rice and curry onto the plates on the table. 'I'm not in the mood.'

Emma crossed over to the sink with a clean glass from the cupboard and put it under the tap. She flipped the lever and water spewed into the glass, spraying her face in the process. She yelped and stumbled back, straight into Lauren who had run to her aid.

'I should have warned you about that tap,' Lauren said apologetically and gently dabbed Emma's face with a napkin.

Emma's cheeks were stained red. 'It's okay.'

Does she know how gorgeous she looks when she blushes? As hard as Lauren tried not to, she imagined the flush on Emma's cheeks in the afterglow of making love to her. Fire raced through her blood as she thought of what it would be like to lie naked with her. A slow, throbbing desire moved through her, but this wasn't the best time to let her imagination run wild. She averted her gaze, afraid of what Emma might see in her eyes, then stepped away from her and gestured at the table.

'We better eat before our food gets cold,' Lauren said, ignoring the ache that had settled between her thighs.

'I suppose we should,' Emma said. 'I'll just get you that drink.'

Tentatively lifting the tap lever this time, she filled the glass with water and joined Lauren at the table.

'You know, I'm getting used to this,' Emma said, toying with her food.

Lauren noticed the sadness in her eyes and guessed what she was thinking; her own thoughts were the same. Time was moving so fast. In just over a week she would be back in Paris.

'Me too,' Lauren said, knowing full well she would

be as hurt as Emma if, or when, the time came to say goodbye.

'At least we saw each other again,' Emma said half-heartedly.

'Yes, there is that.'

They ate the rest of their meal in silence. Tiredness stung Lauren's eyes, and despite not wanting to part with Emma so soon, the long day had caught up with her. She pushed her plate away and started to clear the table.

'I'm taking a shower then calling it a night. I'm knackered.'

Disappointment flickered across Emma's features. 'Okay. Don't worry about the plates. I'll load the dishwasher.'

'Are you sure?'

Emma scraped the remains of her food into the rubbish bin. 'Yes. Now go. If it's not too late and Mike accepts my friend request, do you want me to let you know?'

'Yes.'

***

After her shower, Lauren slipped between the covers, naked. The sheets were cold against her skin. She imagined entwining her body around Emma—

Don't even go there.

By the time Lauren drifted to sleep, Emma hadn't knocked.

Chapter Twenty

Emma had awoken an hour before and was on her second cup of coffee. The familiar sound of her Facebook notification had slid into her subconscious, rousing her from her slumber. Seeing that Mike had accepted her friend request, it had been impossible to go back to sleep. If it hadn't been six o'clock, she would have woken Lauren right there and then. Instead she'd contained herself by keeping an eye on Mike's location and tracking him to his workplace—just where they needed him to be.

At seven thirty, Emma couldn't wait any longer. She hurried down the hallway, tapped on Lauren's door, and thrust it open with more energy than she'd intended.

Lauren jerked awake with a start, the duvet falling away from her body, revealing perfectly formed breasts. Emma's breath caught in her throat. Unable to tear her eyes away, she rushed her hand up to cover them.

'I am so sorry.'

'It's okay.' The sexiness of Lauren's husky morning voice didn't help the situation.

An unexpected throb below Emma's waist made her grateful she wasn't a man. Her instant desire would have been difficult to disguise.

'It's just that, um, Mike accepted my friend request.'

Stop thinking about her breasts, Emma repeated over

and over in her head.

Lauren sounded alert when she asked, 'Can you see his location?'

With her eyes still covered, Emma nodded. She heard the quilt ruffle and the sound of light footsteps. Two thoughts crossed her mind. One: *Is she completely naked?* Two: *Will she notice if I peek?*

'You can uncover your eyes. I'm decent.'

Emma lowered her hand, disappointed to see a white dressing gown covering Lauren's body, though the white fabric suited her slight olive complexion.

Lauren pulled her hair into a bundle on top of her head and expertly clipped it into place. Emma's eyes were drawn to her cute ears, and she fought the urge to reach out and caress them as Lauren walked passed.

'I'm going to take a shower,' Lauren said. 'Mike must be on an early shift.'

When Emma had first broached the idea of confronting Mike, Lauren doing it alone hadn't been part of her agenda. 'I really don't like the idea of you going alone.'

'I promise if I feel like I'm in any danger, I'll scream like a banshee,' Lauren said lightly.

'Just make sure there are people around to hear.'

'I promise.' Lauren looked back at her. 'I can't thank you enough for doing all this.'

'Please don't get any ideas about me being Mother Teresa. I'm kind of hoping this gets sorted so I can persuade you to move back to London.'

Lauren smiled. 'Let's hope this is the beginning of

the end.'

Emma left shortly after, the image of Lauren's breasts foremost in her mind. Two hours later, the memory was still vivid as she sat in her office, gazing out of the window, daydreaming.

Gina walked in without knocking, and she wasn't happy. *Does she know about me visiting Louise?*

'Is everything all right?' Emma asked innocently.

'No. No, it's not. You've got a visitor, he said he's here to talk to you about Louise. I hope this isn't the person who attacked her, Emma.'

Emma looked at the door then heard the familiar sound of Jay's voice.

Shit, I forgot to call him. Which wasn't surprising, seeing as Lauren had been occupying her every thought.

'Gina. It's a long story, but trust me on this I know what I'm doing.'

'I don't like this one bit, Emma. You shouldn't be involved with this person, not while the situation with Louise hasn't been resolved.'

Emma was about to say that Louise had admitted Jay hadn't attacked her, when she realised she would be outing herself.

'I'll talk to him,' Emma said. 'And I'll make sure he doesn't come here again.'

With Gina's anger sated, Emma grabbed her jacket and went to find Jay.

Emma spotted him in conversation with Jack in the corridor and told him, 'Come on. Follow me.'

Outside, she waited until they were away from the

building before stopping.

'You look pissed off.' Jay thrust his hand in his pocket and withdrew a packet of cigarettes. Tapping the packet, he took one out and shoved it between his lips before lighting it.

'I am, to be honest. You shouldn't show up at my workplace without—'

'You said you'd call me.'

'I know I did. I meant when I had something useful to tell you.'

She watched silently as he took a drag from the cigarette. 'So you haven't spoken to Louise then?'

'Let's talk over there,' she said, pointing to a wooded area across the street. They walked on in silence until they reached a small bench under an oak tree with barren branches. Emma sat down, but Jay remained standing.

Jay flicked his cigarette on the ground. 'So?'

'So?'

A petite woman with dirty blonde hair walked by with her German Shepherd puppy. The dog lunged towards Emma and jumped up on her lap with large, muddy paws. Embarrassed, the owner tried to tug him away, but to no avail.

'Sabre, bad boy,' the woman said.

Emma laughed as Sabre nestled his head against her stomach. She didn't mind getting dirty. It was only mud.

'It's okay,' Emma said. 'He's absolutely adorable.'

The woman snorted. 'Adorable? I've only had him

a week and he's managed to destroy my best pair of shoes and wrecked my sofa. And don't get me started about him keeping me up all night.'

'Sounds like a naughty kid,' Jay said, reaching over and ruffling the dog's fluffy fur.

'And then some.' The woman gave one final tug on the lead and Sabre leapt down. 'Come on. Home time for you.'

The woman trotted behind Sabre as he dragged her towards a tree.

'She's got her hands full with him,' Emma said, chuckling.

'Yeah,' Jay agreed, lighting up another cigarette.

Emma's eyes narrowed. 'They're bad for you, you know.'

'Yeah, I'm going to give them up once this situation with Louise is sorted,' he said and took a deep pull. He slowly released a great plume of grey smoke.

Sitting there, she struggled to understand why Louise hadn't felt comfortable enough to discuss Jay with her. She thought she'd provided Louise with a safe haven to open up in and speak honestly about her life. Obviously, Emma had been wrong. She studied Jay and wondered where he'd got the strength at his age to stand out in a world of conformists. To stand alone in a society that didn't understand transgender people.

'Sabre, come back here now! Sabre!'

The blonde-haired woman chased after her puppy, who had broken free from his lead and was legging it across the park. Her shrill voice faded as she disappeared into the woods.

Jay looked at the unfolding scene with concern. 'Do you think I should help?'

'They'll be fine. The direction he's going in doesn't lead anywhere. He'll have to stop a bit further up. She'll catch up with him at the other end.'

'If you say so.'

Emma pulled her jacket tighter around her chest as a cold gust of wind blew over her. Crossing her legs, she looked up at Jay, who was puffing on the cigarette for dear life.

'Do you mind telling me how you met Louise?' she asked, genuinely interested about their relationship.

A grin grew on his face, and Emma couldn't help but smile too. She knew exactly what it was like to have the person you loved make you brim with happiness.

'A few weeks ago at a party. She was with her friends, and I was alone most of the night.' His eyes clouded over as though he were reliving the night. 'I spilt a drink on her by accident. She was wearing a white silk top her mum had bought her. Any other person I know would have freaked out, but not Louise. She said the stain added character to the blandness of it.'

'That sounds like Louise,' Emma said, thinking back to the conversations they'd shared over the months. Louise wasn't like most teenage girls whose main motivations in life pertained to boys, clothes, and iPhones. Louise was more interested in finding herself and exploring the world around her.

'Do you mind if I sit down?' Jay asked. He flicked

his cigarette on the floor and stamped on it. 'My ribs start hurting if I stand for too long.'

'No, of course not.' She shuffled to the edge of the bench and Jay slowly sat, wincing in pain. 'You were saying?'

'What? Oh yeah.' Jay ran a hand through his hair. 'Yeah, so after I spilt the drink on her, I said I'd walk her home so she could change. Her friends were over her like a rash, warning her off me and telling her she was a freak if she had anything to do with me. They said this blatantly in front of me, calling me a weirdo and shit like that.'

'That must have been very hurtful,' Emma said. *So that's why Louise's friends were laughing at her and calling her names. Because of her association with Jay. Why didn't she just tell me the truth?*

'Believe me, I've heard people call me worse, so what they were saying wasn't worth jack shit.' Jay laughed briefly. 'If you could have seen the looks on their faces when she walked out with me. Man, it was priceless.'

'And you became close after that?' Emma asked.

'Yeah. She's the only person my age I can talk to.' Jay took his cigarette packet from his jacket, but instead of taking one out, he repeatedly turned the packet over between his fingers. 'She doesn't judge or nothing.'

'I can imagine. Louise is a very lovely person.'

'She's more than that.' His voice wobbled. 'She's the only reason I haven't topped myself.'

'Are you speaking hypothetically?' Emma had

already switched into her counsellor mode, though she couldn't imagine Jay on a therapist's couch. He struck her as someone who liked to carry his troubles alone, letting a select few in. Her thoughts turned to Lauren. *Just like someone I know.*

Jay threw her a cautious look, one that told Emma he was weighing how much he should share.

'I wish I was,' he said. He must have realised Emma was a friend, not a foe, and someone he could let his guard down with. 'There are days when I don't see the point in carrying on. Everyone hates who I am.'

Emma wanted to touch his hand to reassure him, but she refrained. It didn't seem appropriate; Jay was simply stating his feelings in a detached manner, and his demeanour didn't call for sympathy.

'I'm sure that's not true. They can't hate who they don't know.'

Jay scowled despite his injuries. 'My so-called friends don't have a problem taking the piss out of me for no reason other than I'm different.'

'And what about your parents?'

His face relaxed. 'Oh, they're cool. I was really scared to tell my dad, but he's been great. He takes me down to the pub for a drink. He has no problem introducing me to his mates as his son.'

'I'm glad to hear that.'

Jay rubbed the back of his neck and said in a wavering voice, 'Which is why I don't understand why Louise is scared to tell her parents about me.'

'Maybe she knows they won't be accepting.'

'But they'll end up losing her. I'm moving out of the area soon and she's coming with me. Well she was before all this happened.'

Emma coughed into her hand. This was another thing Louise had failed to mention during their sessions. 'And what are your plans for the future?'

Jay shrugged. 'I dunno.'

'University? A job?'

'I said I don't know!' He leant back and folded his arms.

She had touched a raw nerve and knew why. When people were in love, they didn't want to face reality. If anybody knew that, it was Emma. But there was a difference: she could afford to live with her head in the clouds. She had an education, a job, an apartment. What did these kids have? Nothing, not yet anyway, and she wouldn't be doing Jay and Louise justice if she didn't sprinkle a little reality stardust on their plans before they made a big mistake.

'Can you understand why I sound a little apprehensive?' Emma hoped she wasn't coming off as the enemy.

'What? Because we don't want to go to uni?' Jay got to his feet, his nostrils flaring.

'Maybe, maybe not,' Emma said, keeping her tone neutral. 'But you both have to think with your heads on straight. Life out there is tough, Jay.'

He stared down at Emma with a snarl on his lips. 'You think I don't know that?'

'I can only imagine what your life has been like up

until now. How do you think you'll fare once you're on your own without your parents' roof over your head?'

'As long as we're together, none of that shit matters.'

'That's where you're wrong. It matters, and it matters a lot. How long do you think your rose-coloured glasses will last when your stomachs are empty and you have nowhere to live?'

'Why are you talking like this? You're on their side, aren't you? You're just like them.'

He started to back away.

'Jay, please wait. Hear me—'

'I don't want to hear anything from you!' he shouted. 'I thought we could trust you.'

'You can, but that doesn't mean I won't tell you the truth,' Emma said, raising her hands. 'Just think about what I said.'

'Whatever.' He turned and ran towards the main road.

I hope I wasn't that pig-headed as a teenager.

If she thought nailing down a stalker was bad, convincing a teenager he was making a mistake was another matter altogether. She would give Jay a couple of days to calm down then try again, using a different tactic. Hopefully by then she would have spoken to Louise again.

Standing, she hoped Lauren's morning had gone better.

Chapter Twenty-One

This time tomorrow, it will all be over, Lauren reminded herself as she manoeuvred the car into the same parking bay as yesterday. This time, however, her nerves were getting the better of her. Today wasn't a case of *if* she bumped into Mike, but when. She didn't know how long it would take to find him, and she had to admit a small part of her wished she wouldn't. What would she do if he freaked out or attacked her? She had the self-defence skills to ward off an initial attack, but what if he had a knife?

Cool your jets, Lauren. Stop getting ahead of yourself. Admit you're scared and be done with it. She inhaled deeply. *Okay, I'm scared, but fear won't stop me.*

Her hand trembled as she found the door handle and pushed the door open. *Stop thinking about it and just do it.*

Before she knew it, she was walking towards Tesco's entrance, shoulders held back, her outer appearance not belying her anxiety.

Something she could only liken to a sixth sense made her turn around, and her heart jumped into her throat. Under a canopied tunnel, Mike pushed along a row of trolleys. Her first instinct was to run back to her car and drive away as fast as possible. To put as much distance between them as she could. *And then what? Keep living like this? Not a chance in hell.*

Buoyed by her anger, she marched in his direction and then stopped, waiting for him to notice her.

When he did, surprise glinted in his eyes. 'Hey, Lauren. I thought I'd bump into you again.'

Even though he was at least ten feet away, she could sense a sinister vibe coming off him.

'This isn't fate, Mike,' she said, trying to keep her voice steady.

Mike stepped away from the trolleys and approached her. Lauren glanced around, grateful there were plenty of people nearby.

'Of course it is,' he said. 'When you dropped out of school, I never thought I'd see you again. But here you are, in the flesh, and as sexy as ever.'

He paused, as if waiting for her reaction. She wanted to slap him so hard that he would come to his senses and realise what he had done to her.

'Do you want to go out for a drink later? I finish work at two. We can—'

'This isn't a social call, Mike.'

His eyes narrowed. 'Then what is it?'

'I want you to leave me the fuck alone.' She pulled out the notes from her pocket and threw them at him.

Her stomach flipped when he didn't even give them a cursory glance as they fell to his feet.

'You know there's a fine for dropping litter around here?'

'Is that all you've got to say now that I've exposed you, little man?'

He slowly bent down and scooped up the notes

but remained silent after he'd examined them. Then he crumpled them in his hand and pushed them into his jacket pocket. 'I get it. You think I sent these to you.'

Anger boiled inside her, but somehow she managed to keep it from spilling over. 'Way to go, Sherlock.'

'How did you know where I was working, Lauren?'

'You're not the only one who knows how to stalk people.'

'Stalk?' He laughed. 'You shouldn't go around saying things like that. People will think you're crazy.'

'Crazy, huh? Well the police didn't think I was crazy this time round, Mike. You got away with this shit years ago, but it won't be that easy this time.'

'What are you talking about?'

'I know you stalked me at school and you're doing it again. Play innocent if you like.' Lauren had planned on telling him the effect he'd had on her life, but he'd likely get off on hearing what a good job he'd done. Instead she dug into her pocket for the paper from the police station. She held it close enough to his face so he could read it. 'You see this? I reported you to the police. They have your name and they know exactly what you've been up to.'

He took a threatening step towards her. 'You shouldn't have done that. You really shouldn't have.'

'You don't scare me. Not now that I know who you are. You're a pathetic excuse for a human being.' She tightened her hand around her car key, grateful for the security it provided. 'Just remember: you started all this. If you come anywhere near where I live again, I'll have you arrested. Don't say I didn't warn you.'

Mike's mouth dropped open, and she decided that was as good a time as any to leave. Her legs felt weak, but she walked strong and tall—until she reached her car. Leaning her full weight against it, she fiddled with the key and inserted it into the lock.

Her breath was laboured as she rested her forehead against the steering wheel. She had done it. *Let's hope that puts an end to it.*

Chapter Twenty-Two

Emma had been on tenterhooks all day thinking about Lauren's confrontation with Mike. Due to back-to-back appointments, she barely had time to use the loo, let alone call Lauren for an update. By the time she was on her way home she realised the battery on her mobile was dead. Frustrated, she headed straight to Lauren's.

Lauren sat at the kitchen table as Emma made two cups of tea before joining her.

'Come on then. I want all the details,' Emma said and set a cup of tea in front of her.

Lauren nodded in thanks. 'It was pretty much what I expected. I accused him, and he hardly said anything. I mouthed off a bit and he tried to look all menacing. All in all, it was a bit anticlimactic.'

'In what way?'

'All these years I've held this stereotypical image of what my stalker would be like, you know? Some guy with a crazed look in his eyes, living in his mum's basement, with defaced pictures of me covering the walls.' She paused momentarily. 'And then standing there with Mike, coming face to face with my actual nightmare—I felt stupid for running away all those years ago.'

'Don't beat yourself up about it. For all you knew he could have been a maniac. If I'd been in your shoes, I think I would have reacted the same way. Besides, it hasn't been all bad. You've carved yourself a fantastic career.'

'I suppose.'

'It's over now, so you can relax and get ready for your exhibition with peace of mind.'

'Just hearing you say that is like music to my ears.'

The letterbox sounded and Emma and Lauren stared at each other, startled.

Emma was sure Lauren was thinking the same thing as her.

'I'm sure it's a takeaway leaflet or something,' Emma said, trying to make light of the situation. 'I'll see what it is. Might be something we can order tonight.'

'Thanks.'

In the hallway, a lone envelope lay on the floor. Emma rushed to pick it up and turned it over in her hand. It was addressed to Lauren, and she knew exactly who had sent it. Without thinking, she opened the door and stepped out into the hallway, looking left and right. Empty. Pulling the door shut behind her, she took off towards the lift. Someone was in it and the arrow was pointing downwards. With the determination of an athlete going for gold, Emma took the stairs, jumping them three at a time and using the rail to keep her balance. If she caught Mike, she would call the police. Ten floors down, she stopped for a few seconds to catch her breath before starting down again. Fifth floor—she was so close. She prayed she wasn't too late as she reached the ground floor and ran to the lift.

Bent over, hands on her knees and panting like a

runner who just finished a five-kilometre marathon, she waited. Despite having the fitness level of a couch potato, she had beaten the lift. A soft ping announced its arrival. Emma straightened. The door slid open to reveal … an elderly lady and her dog.

Damn! Emma slapped her thigh and ran outside, frantically looking up and down the street. She knew it was pointless. Mike was long gone. Disgruntled, she returned to Lauren's apartment.

'Are you trying to scare the life out of me?' Lauren asked. 'Why did you run out of here?'

'This came.' She threw the letter on the table.

'Is it …?'

'Looks like it. Do you want me to open it?'

Lauren nodded.

Ripping the envelope open with more force than necessary, Emma fished inside and pulled out the paper. 'It's blank.'

'Let me see.' Lauren took the envelope from her. 'There's no stamp so it was definitely hand delivered. So he's managed to enter the apartment block again, despite the building management asking the other residents to be more vigilant.'

'I know, security here is a joke. It's also obvious he doesn't want you to have a copy of his handwriting. That's probably why he kept the letters you gave him.'

'I'm such a bloody idiot. It didn't even cross my mind.'

Emma took her phone from her pocket and tapped on the Facebook app. She went to Mike's page and checked for his whereabouts.

'Just as I thought.'

'What is it?'

'Mike's unfriended me. He must have put two and two together.' Taking Lauren by the shoulders, she said, 'Listen to me. He's harmless. He's blowing hot air. He wants to scare you, but he won't beat us. We have to be smarter, that's all.'

'How?'

'By catching him in the act. Once we have hard evidence, the police will have to do something.'

'But how are we going to get evidence?'

'I think I know just the thing.' She glanced at her watch. 'If we leave now, we'll make it to the shop before it closes. Get your jacket on.'

'Where are we going?'

'You'll see.'

***

Every day on her way to work Emma passed Spyware, and it had never entered her mind that she would one day be going there to buy something, but here she was with Lauren at her side, watching the owner, Johnny—a man with thick, black, wiry hair and the bushiest eyebrows she had ever seen—give them a demonstration.

'This little baby is one of the best cameras on the market.' Johnny attached a camera the size of a pinhead to the button on his black shirt. 'Take a look at the screen over there.'

They followed his gaze and saw themselves on a TV monitor. The women gasped at the clarity of the picture. It was perfect for what they needed.

'Why aren't cameras like that used in CCTV instead of the low-quality ones we have all around London?' Emma asked.

'It all boils down to money,' Johnny said.

'Surely it's worth it if you can get a clear shot of a perpetrator rather than have police waste their time trying to identify the person.'

'You're preaching to the converted, sweetheart. And these cameras aren't just great at catching criminals. They're also good at catching husbands when they're getting up to no good. I'll tell you a true story.'

Before Emma could point out they were in a rush, he began his tale of a woman who had bought the camera to spy on a nanny she suspected wasn't looking after her baby properly.

His eyes shone with glee as he reached the end. 'Imagine her surprise when she played back the footage and there was her hubby going at it with the nanny.'

Emma was uninformed on the etiquette of hearing the torrid details of a cheating partner. Was she meant to laugh because the wife had caught the husband using the shop owner's camera, or at the situation as a whole?

Unsure what to do, she widened her eyes and said, 'No kidding?'

'I swear on my wife's life, I'm not lying. The customer came back with her friends to see what else I had for them. Women. You can't live with them, but you sure as hell can't live without them.'

Emma and Lauren exchanged glances.

'We'll take that camera,' Emma said, retrieving her purse from her bag.

'You don't have to pay. I can afford it,' Lauren said and patted down her jacket.

'So can I, so don't worry about it.' She handed her debit card to Johnny, and he put the transaction through the till.

'Thank you. I don't know why I didn't think of this myself,' Lauren said once Johnny had disappeared through a door behind the counter.

'That's what you have me for.' Emma smiled. 'I told you I'd look after you, and I am.'

Johnny reappeared, put the camera box in a bag, and handed it to her. 'If you ever need anything, you know where I am. Good luck, ladies.'

'We aren't the ones who'll need it if this camera works,' Emma said, but Johnny had already moved on to help another customer.

As Emma put her card away, her mobile phone pinged with a text message. Taking it out of her pocket, she scrolled down to the message and read it. 'Hope wants to meet up for drinks tonight down on Oxford Street. Are you up for it?'

'Not really. She can come over to ours—I mean my place if she likes,' Lauren replied.

'Cool.'

Emma texted her back:

Come round to Lauren's.
We're going James Bond style

Within seconds, her phone pinged again.
Come again?

Emma let out a breath as she typed:
We bought a security camera to catch Lauren's stalker.

Hope responded:
K. See you later
X

Emma stuffed her phone back into her pocket as they left the shop. 'If the security camera doesn't catch Mike in action, it's on to Plan B.'

'What's that then?'

Emma laughed and looped her arm through Lauren's. 'I'll let you know when I think of it.'

***

Back at Lauren's apartment, Emma wasn't surprised to find Fiona hanging around outside Lauren's door. She didn't strike Emma as the type who gave up easily, but Emma couldn't think of her as a stalker. She was too brazen and in your face to play those kinds of games. Emma doubted Fiona would ever be so cowardly as to torment Lauren from afar, seeing as she had no qualms about bothering her in person.

Fiona eyed them with curiosity as they approached. 'You've 'ad a nice day, I take it?'

'Hardly,' Lauren said, unlocking the door. 'We've been out buying a security camera.'

'Pardon? A security camera?' Fiona said.

'To catch the person who is putting letters through my letterbox,' Lauren said as though she were relaying information to a five-year-old.

'Ah, but I thought you knew who it was. You were wrong, no?' Fiona said triumphantly.

'No, it's the same person, but he hasn't got the message of how serious I am about pressing charges, but to do that I need evidence. Hence the camera.'

'I need to speak with you.' Fiona looked at Emma then back at Lauren. 'Alone.'

'In that case, I'll be off,' Emma said and backed away down the hall. 'Are we still doing drinks tonight?'

'Definitely,' Lauren said. 'I can't wait. I'll see you around seven?'

'Sure thing.'

The resentment in Fiona's eyes was palpable but her voice sounded reasonable as she said, 'Bye, bye.'

She smirked at Emma, but shock soon replaced her smug look when Lauren said, 'You've got five minutes, Fi. I have a ton of work to catch up on.'

Emma poked her tongue out at Fiona then ran to the lift. She knew it was childish, but she felt as anxious and giddy as a child at Christmas, wondering if she'd get the present she wanted more than anything. In this case, the present was the woman of her dreams. Now that

Lauren could come home to London and feel safe again, was there a chance of them getting together? Though Lauren reciprocated her attraction, was it enough to give up her life in Paris?

Chapter Twenty-Three

'I don't appreciate your behaviour around Emma,' Lauren said, casting Fiona a look of annoyance.

'Emma, Emma, Emma, that's all I keep 'earing from you. What about us?' Fiona pouted, her normally thin lips more than doubling in size.

Lauren procured a beer from the kitchen then retreated to the sofa, swallowing down a scream. 'Fiona, please get it through your head! There is no "us". This has to stop. I want you to leave me alone.'

'You don't really mean that.'

Lauren looked up at her. 'I really do, Fi.'

Fiona chewed on her bottom lip, deep in thought. 'You're really not going to forgive me for my … little indiscretion, are you?'

'Has it only taken seven months for that to sink in?' Lauren flopped back against the sofa and took a long lug of her drink.

'I thought we were stronger than this.'

'We were, until you felt the need to cheat on me. I told you at the very beginning that if you broke my trust, that was the end of it. There was no going back. Yet you decided to do it anyway, and now you have the cheek to make our break up all about me, as if I'm the one who caused all the problems.'

'Are you saying you wouldn't get back with me even if Emma wasn't here?'

'How does what you're saying even make sense? We haven't been in a relationship for seven months, and Emma's just come back on the scene.'

'Because I know you. I know you need me—'

'Need you? That's just it. I might have thought I did, but these last few days have taught me that I am strong. Despite everything—the letters, the burglary—I haven't run. I'm still here.'

'With Emma.'

'Oh give it a rest. In fact, I'm done talking about us—for good.'

Fiona suddenly took the conversation in another direction. Sheepishly she said, 'I came to tell you I'm moving to Rome.'

'Isn't that where your floozy lives? I assumed she'd dumped you.'

Fiona averted her gaze, a flush of crimson rising up her neck and covering her face. 'No she didn't. I 've just been thinking a lot and decided I was going to choose you and stay in Paris, but I can see there's no point. I only 'ope that one day, when you realise what you've lost—'

'Please, stop pretending what we had was something special. You were never this sentimental about our relationship when we were together. What's changed?'

Fiona stepped towards the sofa, and Lauren held up her hand to stop her.

'I didn't realise what I 'ad with you until it was too late.'

'And there you have it. Too late.' Lauren's heart

softened at the regret in Fiona's eyes. Yes, she'd cheated, and Lauren had no intention of ever taking her back, so there was no point in holding on to any resentment over her betrayal. 'Fi, I hope this relationship works out for you. I really do.'

Then Fiona was gone. *Another door closes.* For good this time, Lauren hoped.

Once Lauren was alone she polished off her beer. For the first time in a long while, work was the furthest thing from her mind. She wanted to open her window and scream as loud as she could that she was free to do whatever the hell she wanted. Free from Fiona and *Mike!* What a low-down, nasty, rotten bastard. *How could he do this to me? To take away the best years of my life, and for what? To scare the life out of me?*

How many life experiences had she missed out on? How many friendships had she cut short in fear of it all happening again?

If Emma hadn't been so insistent about staying around, she could have lost her for a second time. Lauren smiled. Emma. Sweet, beautiful, protective Emma. She couldn't wait to tell her the news that she had decided to come home. It wouldn't take much to pack up her meagre belongings in Paris. *I'll see if Emma wants to go to Paris with me for a mini break.*

As she fitted the camera to the peephole on her door, she imagined walking hand in hand with Emma along the Seine, eating lunch opposite the Eiffel Tower, and visiting the Louvre and all the other great attractions Paris had to offer. Satisfied the camera was secured and unsuspecting passers-by wouldn't notice it, she grabbed her jacket and left. She had shopping to do for this evening, and she needed to see Frankie. For the first time in years, she would go about her daily business without having to watch her back, and it felt great!

***

Less than an hour later, Lauren was standing in Frankie's office, having walked there without a care in the world. When she'd heard footsteps running up behind her, she didn't break into a sweat or look for the nearest hiding place. She'd carried on walking tall, head held high—too pumped up on adrenaline to give a toss about anything.

Frankie stared at her speechlessly when she told him how she confronted Mike. His long, slender fingers drummed on his desk. 'Who knew school friends could be so cruel?'

'He wasn't my friend—not ever.' Despite her soaring spirits, a trace of anger rang in her voice. She wanted Mike to pay for what he'd done.

'This calls for a celebratory drink, don't you think?' He pulled open his drawer and withdrew a bottle of brandy.

'Drinking on the job, Frankie? Whatever next?'

'You'd be surprised.' He walked out of the room and returned minutes later with two mugs. He poured two measures and handed one to Lauren. 'So are you still returning to Paris once the show's over? I was thinking of coming to stay with you for a few weeks. Running this place has knocked the stuffing out of me. I didn't count on the exhibition being so time consuming.'

'I'm afraid you're out of luck. You'll have to stay in a hotel.'

His pressed lips into a fine line. 'Is this what it will be like from now on because you have a new girlfriend? I take it she doesn't want me staying with you?'

'Don't be silly. You can't stay with me because I won't be there. That's what I came to tell you. I'm coming home to London. Isn't that great? You can get in touch with those reporters and tell them they can splash my face anywhere they want.'

Frankie's mouth opened then promptly shut again. Eventually, in a strained voice, he said, 'That is good news. The mysterious Vikki Wells comes out.'

'Nope, not Vikki Wells. I want to start using my real name.'

It would be a relief for people to know her by her birth name. She'd lost count of how many times people had called her by her pseudonym, causing her to blank until realising they were talking to her. Those socially awkward mishaps would be a thing of the past.

Frankie stared obstinately at her for a moment. 'Will you go public with your story? It might bring attention to your work.'

Lauren took her time to think about it. She couldn't see what harm it would do, it might even help others who had experienced the same thing.

'Sure, why not? But please don't go overboard. I want my name to be known for my work not for being the victim of a stalker. I will never give Mike control over my life again.'

This time, she'd got lucky. How many others could say the same?

Frankie's non-judgmental glance put her at ease. He took a gulp of brandy then shrugged nonchalantly. 'Like I've always told you: you lead, I'll follow. I'll set you up an interview for tomorrow morning.'

It finally feels like I'm in the driving seat for once. 'Do you fancy coming over to my place for a drink later?'

'Sure. I'll ditch the brandy,' he said, peeking at her hardly touched drink, 'and bring a bottle of champagne to celebrate your metaphorical release from jail.'

'Great! I'll make some dips—'

'Please, don't go to that much trouble for me,' he said and jumped to his feet.

'It's no trouble at all. Besides Emma and her sister are coming too.'

He stared at the ground. 'Emma?'

'Uh-huh.' She moved the mug to her mouth but decided against drinking any more. The overpowering smell nauseated her.

'You know what? I think I'll give it a miss,' Frankie said, avoiding eye contact as he tidied his desk. 'I don't want to interrupt your girlie night.'

Lauren sensed his embarrassment in thinking it would be the two of them alone. She chided herself for not making the arrangements clear from the start.

'Don't be silly. You know I look at you as one of my closest friends.'

'And that's all?'

'Yes, Frankie,' she said with a shake of her head. 'We're friends.'

Lauren didn't like the way he was appraising her, as if the news that she didn't see him as anything more than a friend shocked him. She had no idea why he would feel that way, considering she had never given him the impression she was anything but gay.

'Off you go then. I'm sure you've got lots to do,' he said.

'Aren't you going to come then?'

'I'll pass on this one. Besides, by the sounds of it, you'll be home for good soon. I'm sure we'll see loads of each other … if Emma can spare you.'

'What does that mean?'

'Oh, you know, new love and everything. When you're happy, you generally don't want people raining on your parade.'

'You should know I'm not that sort of person, and I don't think Emma is either.'

'Okay, whatever you say.'

She rested her hand on his. 'I mean it.'

***

During the short walk to the supermarket, Lauren couldn't help but feel a hint of annoyance. She had begun to feel uncomfortable in Frankie's company, especially when Emma was around. Although he wasn't out and out rude towards Emma, Lauren sensed his reservations about her, and Frankie was not a reserved man. She hated to think he still had a thing for her after she had put him straight about her sexuality years ago, when he first became her agent. Since then, he had respected her boundaries.

No, it can't be that. As she entered the shop, she put his behaviour down to his nerves about her exhibition. After all, his reputation was on the line as much as Lauren's was.

Chapter Twenty-Four

'You're just in time,' Lauren said, sweeping her arm towards the table laden with deli-style foods. She skirted the table like a fluttering butterfly as if she couldn't keep still. 'I hope you're hungry. I kind of got carried away.'

'You can say that again.' Hope grabbed a plate and randomly picked up small bites of food.

Worried, Emma watched Lauren through narrowed eyes. She wondered if something had happened between Lauren and Fiona. Dare she think they had rekindled their romance? The thought froze in her brain and she set her rucksack on a chair.

'Are you okay?' she asked Lauren.

'I'm fine. Why wouldn't I be?' Lauren said, frowning.

In a hushed whisper, Emma said, 'I thought maybe you and Fiona—'

'There isn't any me and Fiona. I think she finally got the message.' The corners of her mouth curled as she nodded at Emma's bag. 'Now what have you got there?'

'What she has in there is Scrabble,' Hope said before Emma had a chance to reply.

Lauren pulled back a chair at the table and slumped into it. 'Oh no. I don't think I have the brainpower to play Scrabble.'

'You guys aren't getting out of it that easily,' Emma said.

Hope let out a deep theatrical groan. 'In that case, I think this calls for a very large glass of wine.'

'I'll second that,' Lauren added.

'Come on. You'll both get legless and blame losing on being drunk.'

'Sounds reasonable to me,' Lauren said.

'You two are terrible,' Emma said opening the Scrabble box and laying the board out on the table.

Lauren reached out and grabbed the bottle of red wine in front of her. She twisted off the cap and poured out three glasses. After handing a glass to Emma and Hope, she held hers in the air. 'To the future.'

'Hear, hear,' Emma said. It felt so good to be chilling out with Lauren and Hope. This was her idea of a perfect night in. Drinks, laughs, and fun.

'So what does the future hold for you now that you have your stalker problem sorted? Well nearly sorted— he hasn't been arrested yet right?' Hope asked as she settled into her seat and munched on a celery stick.

Emma held her breath, not wanting to hear Lauren's answer.

'Hopefully it's only a matter of time and anyway I feel safe knowing who it is. As for the future, I've decided to move back to London.'

Emma had been so distracted by her thoughts that she nearly missed what Lauren had said. 'Did I hear you right?'

'You sure did.'

Emma looked at Hope then back at Lauren. 'I think you're doing the right thing.'

Act normal, she told herself. *How can I act normal when I just found out the woman of my dreams is coming home?*

If Fiona had been there, she would have kissed her feet for making it possible for Lauren to stay by not appreciating what she had. Fiona was firmly in her good books, even though she was the scariest person Emma had ever met.

Lauren laughed. 'And you're not in any way biased?'

Feigning shock Emma replied, 'Me? No way.'

'I believe you, though plenty wouldn't.'

'Are we going to play this sodding game or not?' Hope said, snatching the bag of tiles from the box and picking out her letters.

'Eager much?' Emma said, Hope's change in attitude taking her by surprise. She knew Hope wasn't originally happy about Lauren's reappearance in her life but she thought they had moved past that.

An uncomfortable silence settled between them as Emma and Lauren picked their tiles and rearranged the letters on their trays.

'Here we go,' Lauren said, laying the tiles down on the board.

'Get real. Bawd isn't a word,' Hope said, flicking Lauren's letters off the board.

'It is so.'

'Tell her, Emma,' Hope said.

'How about I look in the dictionary?'

'Please do,' Lauren said, picking up an olive and popping it into her mouth.

'Here we go … Bawd is actually a word. It means

a woman in charge of a brothel. Lauren's right. Sorry.'

'See,' Lauren said and gave Emma a high five.

Hope scraped her chair back as she stood, her eyes squinted and mean. 'I came here for some fun tonight, not to bore myself with Scrabble and watch you two fawn over each other.'

Emma blinked as if she hadn't heard correctly. 'Eh? What the hell are you talking about?'

'Don't play innocent with me.' Hope glared at Lauren. 'Ever since she came back, she's all you've had time for.'

'That's really not fair,' Emma said adamantly. 'I've been helping Lauren. Nothing's been going on between us. And we weren't fawning over each other. It's called playing around, much like we used to.'

'Yeah, you're right there: used too. Don't worry, I'll get out of your hair and let you enjoy the rest of your evening together. I don't know why you bothered inviting me in the first place.'

'Because you're my friend,' Lauren said.

'And my sister,' Emma added. 'Come on, Hope, please sit down. We'll pack the game away and talk instead.'

Hope made no attempt to hide the hurt in her voice as she said to Emma, 'Now you're patronising me. I'm leaving.'

She slipped her arms into her jacket and roughly yanked the zip up.

'Then I'm coming with you,' Emma said and started to rise.

'Don't bother. Seriously, I just want to be alone.' Hope strode from the room, and shortly after, the front door slammed shut.

'What the hell was all that about?' Lauren asked.

Emma shrugged. The only thing that could explain Hope's behaviour was stress from work. It had to be. Hope had been acting stranger than usual these last few days, and Emma knew she had been under pressure since starting the *Wedding Daze* contract. Hope obviously thought Emma should be supporting her, but Emma had been so wrapped up in her need to protect Lauren that she had completely forgotten about Hope. A pang of guilt sliced through her.

'She's under a lot of stress. I'll go and see her tomorrow and take her out for lunch. You can come if you like.'

Lauren circled the rim of her glass with her fingertip. 'I don't think that's a good idea. I'm infringing on her space enough as it is.'

'In what way?' Emma asked, unable to tear her gaze away from the slow caress of Lauren's finger around the glass. If she could have swapped places with the wineglass, she would have in a heartbeat.

'I don't know. Maybe Hope doesn't like sharing you.'

'You make me sound like an entrée,' Emma said, heat rising in her face.

Lauren picked up a sliced carrot, dipped it into a bowl of hummus, and took a bite. 'You do look delicious enough to eat.'

'You think?' Emma's eyes were fixated on Lauren's mouth as she slowly chewed.

'Most definitely.'

Emma moistened her lips. 'Flattery will get you everywhere.'

'That's what I was hoping.'

Emma's hand shook as she wiped a spot of dip from the side of Lauren's mouth with her thumb. Holding her gaze, she said, 'So what do you want to do now that the Scrabble party has been spoilt?'

Lauren raised her eyebrows. 'Any suggestions?'

'I might have one.'

A devilish look entered Lauren's eyes as she moved her chair closer, leaving no room between them. 'Do you want to tell me what it is?'

Emma's heart pounded and her breath caught in the back of her throat. 'I'd rather show you.'

This was it, the moment she had been fantasising about for fourteen years, there was no reason to hold back any longer.

Emma kissed the tip of Lauren's nose, then her eyes, and finally her lips. A small breathless whisper escaped her when Lauren's mouth parted and she dipped her tongue between the seams of her lips. She felt lightheaded and dizzy, but when Lauren's tongue grazed hers in a sweet, tentative touch as if testing the waters, Emma's inhibitions were annihilated.

Reaching over, Emma wrapped her arms around Lauren's waist and pulled her onto her lap. Lauren straddled her, her arms encircling Emma's neck and her perfect, trim body pressing against Emma's longer frame.

They fit perfectly together—just like Emma had always known they would. Lauren sighed into the kiss, and a well of tears burnt Emma's eyes.

Pulling away, she looked at Lauren. Her lips were swollen and her eyes were darker, laced with desire that heated their depths. A wild, crazy hope blazed through her, but she needed Lauren to be sure. This couldn't be a fling. Her heart couldn't take it.

'Are you sure about this? I—'

'Shh, don't worry. I'm back for good.'

Lauren kissed her again, and this time, Emma didn't question it. Her hands slipped underneath Lauren's shirt and pushed it up. Lauren moaned and tugged at Emma's t-shirt, her bare breasts greeting Lauren as she pulled the t-shirt over Emma's head.

With a tremulous hand, Lauren cupped Emma's breast. At the feel of her hand on her hot skin, Emma groaned into Lauren's neck. Emma fumbled with Lauren's bra strap but quickly removed it. Desperation and reverence mixed inside her as she took in the sight of Lauren bare before her. Beautiful, small breasts begged for her touch, and the open invitation in Lauren's eyes was enough to make her explode. She laid Lauren on the floor, kissing her, letting her hand travel down her soft, smooth skin. Emma relished the feeling of Lauren surrounding her senses, in awe that she could actually show Lauren how much she loved her.

Without looking away, Emma stripped out of her

jeans before pulling off Lauren's. If Emma had thought Lauren was beautiful before, seeing her naked, the obvious desire blazing in her eyes as she looked at her, her arms open to her, humbled her.

Emma fell into Lauren's embrace, ready to drown in the magnificence of her essence and show Lauren how amazing and precious she found her. She was ready to show her how she'd brought so much light and love into Emma's dark world.

Emma kissed her neck, sucking a little on her skin and savouring the salt of her dried tears. Lauren's heart pulsed under her tongue. Down she went, learning the topography of Lauren's body with her hands, her mouth, and her tongue. Lauren's body quivered under her touch. Her sighs and moans fuelled Emma's desire. Love infused the brush against a nipple, a kiss in the navel, a lick at the back of a knee, and the worship at Lauren's centre—all healing the years of longing and unrequited dreams and bringing them into a new reality. *Together.*

Chapter Twenty-Five

A ringing phone cut through the quiet stillness of the morning. Lying flat on her stomach, Lauren stirred, immediately having vivid flashbacks of their lovemaking the night before. How their entwined bodies had been slick with sweat, skin to skin, coming together as one as she lay hypnotised by Emma's touch, tingling under her fingertips that found their way between her thighs. How Emma's warm, moist tongue had lashed Lauren's taut nipples, rousing a melting sweetness within her. The way Emma had kissed every inch of her body until Lauren was begging for release.

Lauren let out a sigh of contentment when she felt Emma trail her finger along her spine. She slowly opened her eyes, filled with an amazing sense of completeness.

'Good morning, sexy,' Lauren said, smiling lazily.

Emma inched towards her, entwining her leg around Lauren's. 'Morning to you too. How're you feeling?'

'How am I feeling? Like I'm in a dream that I never want to wake up from.' A week ago, making love to Emma had been one of her many fantasies. Now that it was a reality, it didn't feel real. She expected to wake up and realise she had imagined the whole thing.

'Me too.'

'Are you hungry?' Lauren asked.

'For you, yes.' Emma crushed her face against Lauren's chest, pressing her lips to the base of her throat.

'I meant for food.'

Emma lowered her face to Lauren's breast and encircled her areola with the tip of her tongue before lifting her head. 'Are you sure?'

Lauren pressed Emma's head back into her breast and groaned when she sucked at her nipple. 'I suppose food can wait, if you insist.'

'I insist. Luckily for you I've got no appointments today so I'll call work and see if I can take the morning off.'

'Oh crap.' Lauren jerked up into a sitting position and reached for her phone. 'I have an interview at nine.'

Frankie had arranged for her to be interviewed by Georgie Maynard, an arts journalist who had carved a name for herself by interviewing up-and-coming talents. She was often cited as discovering Rayleen Richards, a contemporary artist whose work had been featured at Tate Modern.

'Why didn't you say so? I would've set my alarm,' Emma said.

'I totally forgot. I had more interesting things on my mind.' She planted a kiss on Emma's lips then pushed the covers aside. 'You coming with me?'

Emma was sprawled on her back, exposing her nakedness. 'Only if I can take a shower with you first.'

'Okay, but no naughtiness,' Lauren said, pulling Emma from the bed and down the hallway, towards the bathroom.

Georgie would be interviewing Lauren at Frankie's gallery, at Frankie's insistence. As well as getting publicity for Lauren, he wanted to put his gallery on the map. What better way than having the name of the gallery printed in one of London's most popular art magazines? Lauren had tried to get him to share the interview with her so he could plug his gallery himself, but he declined, stating it would take the attention away from her. He'd insisted he'd be happy just to have his name mentioned.

An hour later, Lauren was sitting in Frankie's gallery. Georgie, a thin woman whose hand wouldn't stop fidgeting with the tip of her pen, got straight down to business.

'So, Lauren—I can call you Lauren, right?'

Noticing the glint in the woman's eye, Lauren knew what was coming next and braced herself. She glanced at Emma, who was sitting behind the Georgie, then nodded.

'You've been working under a pseudonym for many years now. Any particular reason why you're coming out of the shadows.'

Lauren crossed her legs and cupped her knee with her hands. 'Yes, there is, Georgie.' She paused. 'I've been in hiding for fourteen years.'

'In hiding.' Georgie gave a nervous laugh. 'Is this a breaking story?'

'I don't know about that, but I hope my story will help anyone who has been through a similar experience.'

'Which is?'

Lauren took a deep breath. 'I had a stalker when I was sixteen which led me to move to France. Every year he would still send threatening letters or revolting presents to my parents' house on my birthday. When I finally came back to London he found out where I was staying and the threatening letters started again. I have now learnt who the person stalking me is. That's why I'm coming out with my true identity today.'

Georgie's eyes widened. 'That must have been tough. Lauren, I'm sure our readers will be interested to hear how this affected you. Were you threatened?'

'Yes, and because of that, I lived my life in fear. I thought my life was in danger, as well as the lives of my family.' She looked at Emma again. 'And I nearly missed out on having a relationship with Emma.'

'Were the authorities involved in your case?'

'Yes, yes they were.'

'And how did they treat you? Did they take you seriously? I only ask because it's not every day you get people going public about being stalked for fear of reprisals.'

'That's not surprising. It's a difficult decision to make, because you never know if outing the person will make matters worse. I just hope that going public will shame him into stopping this madness as well as helping others who may be in a similar situation.' Lauren's latest experience with the police moved to the forefront of her mind. 'But I would like to say that the police officer who dealt with my case took my concerns very seriously.'

She needed to get that point across so if anyone

reading her story had any doubts about involving the police, they could take it from her that the police would help.

'That sounds very encouraging and I hope that your years of what can only be described as terror, will finally come to an end. Thank you for sharing that with me, Lauren, it must have been tough.' Georgie paused to consult her notes. 'So on to the future. This is your first exhibition in London. How does it feel to be back home?'

'Amazing.' She glanced at Emma. 'Absolutely amazing.'

The interview dragged on for another half an hour. Lauren talked about her parents, her life now, and her personal inspirations. When Georgie finally closed her notebook, Bev, the magazine's photographer, snapped several shots of Lauren in front of her images and outside the gallery entrance. Finally, she took pictures of Lauren and Emma together. Lauren asked to have a look at the shots, and as she scrolled through the images, the love between her and Emma was evident for anyone to see.

Georgie left the interview bursting with excitement at her good luck to be the first reporter to run the story.

'God, I was dreading that, but it wasn't as bad as I'd thought,' Lauren said to Emma as they made their way to Frankie's office.

Molly opened Frankie's office door when Lauren knocked.

'Hi, Molly, is Frankie around?' Lauren asked, looking over Molly's shoulder.

'He popped out for milk while Georgie was interviewing you, but he's been gone for at least half an hour.'

'Okay, no worries. I'll call him on his mobile.'

'He left it in the office. I'll leave a note asking him to call you. I'm meeting my fiancé for brunch.'

'Your fiancé? Oh, I thought you and Frankie …'

Molly's hand flew to her mouth and she let out a small giggle. 'Oh my God. Me and Frankie? You've got to be kidding. He's old enough to be my granddad.'

Lauren suppressed a laugh. He wasn't that old, but she supposed to a twenty-year-old, forty-something was pretty old.

'Thanks, Molly. And thanks for all the hard work you've put into getting this place ready. It looks great.'

'Thanks. I think it looks pretty cool,' she said, glancing around at the framed images on the wall.

A massive table covered with crisp, white linen was pressed up against one wall, and silver and bronze statues of unisex figures holding trays were placed strategically around the room. Lauren assumed drinks would be served on them rather than having a bar. She followed Emma's gaze to a large picture of herself, which had been hung on an otherwise blank wall. Now she had outed herself, Frankie insisted on displaying the image as part of his 'getting to know the artist' collection.

'Can I have that picture when the show's done?' Emma asked, staring at the smiling image. 'I'll put it on the ceiling so you're the first face I see when I wake up in the morning.'

'Aww, how sweet,' Molly gushed. 'If Lauren agrees, I can have it wrapped for you after the show's finished.'

'I don't think she'll need my picture. Not when she has the real thing. See you soon, Molly. And thanks again.' Lauren took Emma's hand and led her to the door.

'So where to now?' Emma asked as they left the gallery.

'Since we missed breakfast, home to feed you.'

'You're a woman after my own heart,' Emma said, nudging her with her head.

The streets were teeming with people, and Lauren and Emma weaved their way through them to cross the road.

'Do you want to take a taxi back?' Lauren asked Emma, hoping she'd say yes. Not because she was fearful in any way. She just wanted to get home as quickly as possible. They had unfinished business to attend to in the bedroom.

'No way. From now on, I want you to enjoy your freedom.' Emma steered them towards a narrow lane. 'Besides I want to wander round the book shop down there.'

'Can we come another day? I'm starving.' She refrained from telling her the real reason for her need to get home.

'Hmm, you do look a little peaky, I suppose.' Emma wiggled her eyebrows. 'And we need our energy up for round two.'

It's amazing that we both think alike. Lauren's hand curved around Emma's waist and she pulled her against her side. 'Exactly.'

Chapter Twenty-Six

Emma's lungs were burning, and her legs weak. She could barely put one foot in front of the other. 'Seriously, Lauren, I think I'm gonna die.'

'Come on, there's only two more floors left.'

'Only!' Emma dropped onto the carpeted step and hung her head between her legs. Between breaths, she said, 'How about I wait here and you go to your apartment and bring me something to eat … as well as an oxygen tank.'

Lauren laughed. 'I did say to take the lift.'

'And miss out on going into cardiac arrest? Where's the fun in that?'

Lauren bent over and kissed the top of her head. 'Do you want me to run up and get you a bottle of water?'

Emma shook her head. 'I'll be all right … in a few hours.'

'I see I was wrong about you. After last night's performance, I thought you had stacks of stamina.'

'Oh, I do, while lying down.' She reached up and drew Lauren's face nearer. 'I think I need the kiss of life.'

'If that's what it takes to get you up those stairs …' Lauren traced her tongue along the outline of Emma's lips before giving her a slow, deep kiss that sent the pit of her stomach into a wild swirl.

Lauren drew back, holding her gaze with half-hooded eyes. 'Better?'

Emma looked upwards for a second, then glanced down again. 'One more should do the trick.'

'I'm afraid you'll have to wait until we get upstairs, unless you want me to tear your clothes off right here.'

Emma's mouth turned down in a delicate pout. 'Spoilsport.'

'We're wasting time. Let's go.'

Emma grabbed the handrail and pulled herself to her feet. She trailed behind Lauren in the hope of conserving her energy and got a perfect view of Lauren's sexy arse in her tight jeans.

They exited the stair well and walked towards Lauren's apartment, debating what should come first: sex or food.

'You expecting a delivery?' Emma asked, noticing a box sitting outside Lauren's front door. When they came to a stop Emma bent over, resting her hands on her knees.

'No. It's probably for the owner—or not.' Lauren picked up the box and opened the lid. 'It's addressed to me.'

'Now you know where Frankie disappeared to. Seems a bit cloak and dagger, doesn't it? He could have just given—' Emma paused when she realised Lauren hadn't moved. 'What is it?'

'A black rose.'

'Who would send you a black rose?' Emma asked.

Lauren handed the box to her with the message

card. Emma scanned the message and adrenaline shot through her.

Time is running out for you Lauren.

'That little shit hasn't learnt his lesson,' Emma said.

'At least we've got him on camera this time.'

They stepped inside the apartment, and Lauren pushed the cable from the security camera into her phone. With Emma leaning over her shoulder, Lauren started the footage a few hours previously and they both peered at the screen as she forwarded through quickly. Emma willed Mike to appear, just to confirm she'd been right about him. Unfortunately, there wasn't much to see, besides the odd neighbour and a cleaner hoovering the hallway.

Their breath caught when a shadow fell on her door. The atmosphere was heavy with tension as they waited for the person who'd delivered the rose to come into view. A man wearing a baseball cap stared back at her. Emma knew straight away it wasn't Mike; the man didn't look anything like him.

'I can't believe it's not him,' Lauren said, her disappointment obvious.

Emma took the phone from Lauren and paused the footage. 'So he didn't deliver the rose himself, but he wasn't too smart either. Look at the logo on the cap.'

Lauren peered at the image and read the name of the florist, 'Petals. Do you know it?'

'No. I'll look it up on my phone. We can pay them a visit after we've seen Mike. Together, this time.'

'Okay,' Lauren conceded. 'But shouldn't we go to the florist first, just to make sure?'

'It makes no difference. I know Mike sent it. If anything, going to the florist is only to confirm he was the sender. I think we have to confront him.'

'If that's what you think,' Lauren said, disconnecting the camera's cable from her phone. 'Let's do it.'

***

It didn't take long to locate Mike rounding up the trolleys in Tesco's car park. Noticing them, he pushed the trolleys aside and waited.

'He doesn't look like he was expecting us,' Lauren whispered as they neared him.

'Maybe he's so thick-skinned he doesn't care.'

'Hey ladies, what a nice surprise,' he said sarcastically. 'You come to buy wine for a quiet night in together? Or a nice Indian meal for two?'

Emma rolled her eyes and continued walking until she was standing in his personal space. She wished she were a six-foot-tall man with big, bulging muscles so she could scare the living daylights out of him. 'No, Mike, we're not here to buy anything. What will it take to get through to you?'

'Do I have to go back to the police?' Lauren asked.

'The police.' He scowled. 'You mean the policeman who came round and basically said you have nothing on me. No evidence, nothing!'

'You're a liar! What did I do to deserve this, Mike?

Did I do something to offend you or hurt you in anyway?'

'Mike, back to work,' a man in a dark suit called out as he walked on the opposite side of the car park. 'You aren't being paid to stand around talking to the customers.'

'All right, Mr Cooper. Just giving the ladies the lowdown on some of Tesco's finest deals,' he called back cheerfully before turning to Lauren and smiling. 'No doubt I'll be seeing you ladies again, real soon.'

Mike returned to the job at hand, pushing the long line of trolleys toward the store's entrance while whistling, 'Heigh-ho, it's off to work we go,' from Disney's *Snow White*.

Emma watched him, unsure what to think of his attitude. Was he lying about the police not even giving him a slap on the wrist? Was it because of the lack of evidence that he felt secure enough to carry on harassing Lauren? None of it made sense. None of it.

She turned to the woman caught in the middle of this and wasn't surprised to see the terror on her face. Lauren thought she had finally seen the light at the end of the tunnel, only to realise it was the light of an oncoming train heading straight for her, full steam ahead.

Emma reached for her, struggling to find words of comfort. They were back to square one, but in a worse position than before. They might have found her stalker, but they couldn't do anything about it. The florist identifying Mike to the police was their last hope.

Chapter Twenty-Seven

Lauren had thought the one-mile walk to the florist would be enough to dispel the adrenaline coursing through her body, but it wasn't. Her nerves were still on edge. Just when the constant chatter and dread had begun to recede, it was back in full force. She should have known it wouldn't be as easy as confronting Mike and him leaving her alone to live happily ever after. *That's how things work in movies, but this is real life—my life, and I have to take control of it.*

Even when Emma was outlining her idea about getting the florist to positively identify Mike, only half of her had been listening—the part that didn't want to leave Emma. The part that wanted to believe she would be safe in London and being with Emma was enough to let her live her life without looking over her shoulder. But the practical side was already making plans to return to Paris.

Or maybe she could travel to India. She'd always wanted to go, and there was no chance of Mike finding her there. She glanced at Emma and her heart jumped into her throat. The look on her face said it all; even she knew it was the end of them, no matter how much she wished it wasn't true.

The shop front of Petals was a muted aubergine colour, with swirly typography on the glass window. As they entered, a pale-faced woman in her thirties, with reddish, limp hair, hung up the phone.

Lauren thought she saw a look of recognition in the woman's eyes when she looked up at them but dismissed it. She'd never seen her before in her life.

The woman brushed an imaginary speck of dirt from her shoulder and addressed Emma. 'Morning, how can I help?'

'Hiya,' Emma said, holding the flower box out in front of her. 'This was delivered earlier. We wanted to know if you could tell us who sent it.'

The woman raised her eyebrows, turned to Lauren, and then back to Emma. 'Is this some kind of joke?'

Emma frowned. 'What do you mean, a joke? I know you can't give us the sender's personal information, but could you at least tell us if they were male or female and gives some kind of description?'

The woman walked around the counter and headed over to a bunch of lilies. She plucked a few from the flower bucket, one at a time. 'Ha ha, very funny.'

'Excuse me?' Emma said.

'Okay, who set this up?'

Emma looked at Lauren, who shrugged. The woman obviously had them mistaken for other people. What else could explain her odd behaviour?

'I'm sorry, but I don't know what you're talking about,' Emma said.

'Oh, I see. It's a surprise for you, and your friend here didn't want to tell you.' She winked at Lauren.

Confused, Lauren said, 'What are you talking about?

What surprise?'

'Do you want me to tell her?'

'Tell who what?' Lauren asked, a little freaked out by the woman, so her tone was sharper than she'd intended.

The woman strode back to her position behind the counter. 'Okay ladies, I don't know what kind of drama you've got going on here, but I'm not getting involved.'

'Look, just tell us what we need to know, and we'll get out of your hair,' Emma said.

'Right. The person who ordered this flower for delivery was her,' she said, pointing at Lauren. 'She came in here yesterday and paid in cash. Asked for it to be delivered today.'

The whole scene was surreal. 'Me?! You must have imagined it. I didn't even know this place existed until today.'

'Are you calling me a liar?' The vein in the woman's forehead throbbed.

'She's not saying that at all,' Emma said assertively, but calmly. 'There must be a mix up. You see, the flower was delivered to her.'

'Yeah, well, there's no mix up. And I don't care where it was delivered. She sent it.'

Laura stood rigid and speechless. *Why would a stranger make that up? Am I going mad? Did I order the rose in some kind of out of body experience without realising it?* After mulling it over for a few seconds, she chided herself. *Don't be so bloody stupid. Of course I didn't.*

'Did somebody get to you? Is this what this is

about? Who is it? Who are you protecting? Tell me!'
Lauren shouted.

'You're obviously crazy and need help. Take this
woman out of my shop before I call the police.' The
woman had a steely glint in her eye as her hand hovered
over the telephone.

Emma took Lauren by the arm. 'That won't be
necessary. We're going.'

Lauren shook her hand off. She couldn't believe
Emma was giving up so easily. What had happened to
the gung-ho show about getting to the bottom of
things? 'But—'

'We'll talk outside,' Emma said firmly and ushered
her out the door.

Out on the pavement, Lauren looked at the florist,
who was staring back at her through the window.

'Emma, you don't believe her, do you?'

'Calm—'

'No, I won't calm down. You wanted angry, now
I'm fucking angry. No, that's an understatement. I'm
fucking fuming. That woman in there is lying.'

'There has to be a logical explanation.'

'Like what? That I have a long-lost twin I know
nothing about? Somehow I'm sure my parents would
have told me.'

Emma shook her head, laughing wryly. 'No, I
don't think you have a twin, but the florist was adamant
it was you.'

'I swear on the Holy Bible I didn't even know this
place existed until you mentioned it.'

'This truly is bizarre.'

'Mike's obviously out to make me look crazy,' Lauren said airily, though she felt sick to her stomach.

'But why?' Emma asked, tilting her head slightly.

'Who knows what makes that sick bastard tick?'

If Lauren didn't know better, she would think Emma actually believed the florist. There was nothing she could do about that. As long as Lauren knew the truth, that was all that mattered. She broke away from Emma and hailed a taxi. *And there I was thinking Emma would be by my side unconditionally.*

Neither woman spoke as they headed back to Vauxhall. Lauren wasn't in the mood to plead her case to deaf ears. If Emma wanted to believe she was stalking herself, so be it.

As they alighted from the cab, Lauren spotted Hope outside her building. *Great, just what I don't need.*

'Hope,' Emma called out.

Hope turned upon hearing her name and gave a small wave. She walked back to the entrance and waited for them.

'I thought you'd be at work, Emma,' she said, fidgeting with her hair as they neared. 'Look, Lauren, I wanted to apologise for my behaviour last night. It was nice of you to invite me round and I was out of order. Work was getting on top of me, I'm sorry.'

'Don't worry about it,' Lauren said.

Emma gave Hope's shoulder a slight squeeze. 'Come back upstairs with us. Maybe you can help us figure out what the hell is going on.'

***

Lauren was glad for the few minutes alone while she walked up to her floor. She didn't see the point in Emma asking for Hope's help in figuring things out. What the hell could Hope contribute in solving the puzzle? *Stop focusing your anger on Emma and Hope.*

She tried to be more upbeat when they congregated in her living room with their coffees. Emma and Lauren sat side by side on the sofa, while Hope stood by the window.

'I'm sorry to have to ask you this, Lauren, but are you on any type of medication?' Hope asked bluntly.

Lauren didn't see a shred of embarrassment on her face. What she did see, though, was a sarcastic smirk.

'Medication? No, I'm not. And even if I were, what does that have to do with me delivering a black rose to myself? I suppose I wrote the creepy notes as well.'

Hope rolled her eyes. 'I didn't say that. I'm just trying to make sense of it. There's no need to get defensive.'

Lauren turned to Emma, who had barely said a word since they'd arrived.

'I'm sorry,' Lauren said. 'I'm just feeling a little jumpy.'

'Which is understandable,' Emma said, encircling her arms around her waist and pulling her close.

Lauren stiffened. Emma still hadn't convinced her that she believed it wasn't her who had sent the rose.

'What do you suggest we do, Hope?' Emma asked.

'For starters, Lauren should move out of this apartment.'

'Move out and go where exactly? Lauren asked.

'You could move in with me,' Emma offered.

'That's the last place you should go. We don't know what Mike's capable of, and I'd prefer it if you didn't put my sister's safety on the line. Why don't you stay in a hotel?'

Why isn't Emma saying anything? Lauren wondered. *Does she think I'm a liability as well? One step forward, ten steps back.*

Before today, Emma had been a hundred percent behind her. Now she seemed to doubt her commitment to help her.

'I have to use the loo,' Lauren said and hurried out of the room before she started crying. She felt well and truly alone.

In the bathroom, she stood in front of the mirror and splashed cold water on her face. *Jesus Christ, was it only this morning I was walking on a cloud, thinking I'd put all this shit behind me?*

She sat on the toilet seat and rested her head against the wall, unable to understand why Emma was acting so strangely.

Realising she couldn't hide out in the toilet all day, she made her way back to the living room, but stopped abruptly at the threshold when she heard Hope's voice behind the slightly closed door. It was low and insistent.

'Have you thought of the possibility that Lauren might be doing this to herself?'

'Don't be so silly,' Emma retorted.

'Think about it. This could be a publicity stunt to draw attention to her exhibition.'

'I can't believe she would do something like that. You'd have to be pretty sick in the head, wouldn't you agree?'

Lauren's heart was pounding. She stood fixed to the spot, terrified to move lest the slightest sound give her away. She was painfully aware that the conversation she was overhearing was not intended for her ears.

'You don't even know her!' Hope said. 'You've been living in cuckoo land for too long, feeding on a fantasy that happened when you were sixteen.'

'Explain why she left school then.'

'Who knows? Could have been anything. All I'm saying is that Lauren isn't the woman you want her to be. If you know what's good for you, you'll keep a wide berth.'

Silence. Lauren covered her mouth to stifle a cry. She couldn't believe what she was hearing. They were talking about her as if she were some kind of psycho. She carried on listening to the conversation, her heart breaking by the minute.

'So you really think she made all this up?' Emma whispered.

'Yes, I do, and you're better off as far away from her as possible,' Hope replied in a normal voice. It was obvious she didn't care whether Lauren heard her.

'Maybe it would be for the best—'

Hope cut in before Emma could finish. 'If you had

listened to me in the first place, none of this would have happened.'

Lauren's fingers touched her parted lips. *Oh my God! Could Emma really think that of me? That I would lie about my past? This is worse than I thought.*

She crept back to the bathroom, flushed the toilet, then walked back to the living room.

It took all her strength to look them in the face when she returned. 'If it's all right with you guys, I think I'll take a nap. I feel drained.'

'Do you want me to stay?' Emma asked.

Lauren gathered the coffee cups. 'I need some space to get my head around all this.'

'Won't you be scared?' Hope asked with a strange edge to her voice.

'No, I won't. I'm beyond scared now.' That, at least, was the truth. She had nothing more to fear. If she wasn't in London, what could Mike possibly do to her?

'I really think I should stay. It's—'

'Emma,' Lauren said, unable to keep her anger under wraps. 'You'd better go to work, I'll be fine.'

'But—'

'Please,' Lauren said with finality. She couldn't bear to look at her. She didn't want to remember Emma like this. The memory she wanted to take with her was the one from the night before, when they were tucked away in their little cocoon, where the harsh reality of life couldn't touch them.

'Can I come by later?'

'Tomorrow would be best,' Lauren said, unsure

whether she could put her plan into action by that evening. She was mentally and physically worn down.

'Will you call me if you need me?' Emma asked and hugged her tightly as if she sensed this would be the last time she held her in her arms.

They broke apart and Lauren looked away. She didn't want Emma to see the tears welling in her eyes. 'Sure. Of course I will.'

Lauren walked them to the entrance, took one last look at Emma, then closed the door. Lauren had returned to London against her better judgement, and she wouldn't ignore her instincts again. Without a second to waste, she ran into her bedroom, pulled open the bedside drawer, and took out her passport, intent on booking the Eurostar back to Paris the next morning.

Chapter Twenty-Eight

'I shouldn't have left her,' Emma said to Hope as they walked over to her apartment block. Something didn't feel right about the way Lauren had held her. It had felt so final. She brushed it off as her reading too much into things, as usual. Lauren knew Emma was on her side and they were united in facing her problem with Mike.

'She wanted to be alone,' Hope said irritably. 'She's probably pissed off you caught on to her plan.'

'You can't really believe she's behind all this?' she said, fully realising how silly Hope's observations sounded. *As if Lauren would put herself through all of this stress.*

'Yes, I really do. She's not the first person to pull a stunt like this to garner attention for a show, and she won't be the last.'

'I don't think so. Not Lauren. She's not that shallow.'

'Like I said, you know nothing about the woman.'

'And you do?'

'I know enough, believe me.'

'If you say so,' Emma said. She knew it was pointless trying to reason with Hope when she was in her 'I know what's right' mood. But she wished Hope would show a little compassion for Lauren's predicament, regardless of her personal thoughts.

Emma's mobile phone vibrated in her pocket. Thinking it was Lauren calling to ask her to return to her apartment, she answered straight away.

'Hello?'

'I'm not interrupting anything, am I?' Gina asked.

Disappointment surged through her. 'No, what's up?'

'Do you know what time you'll be in?'

'I'm just on my way, is everything all right?'

'I don't know. Louise's mum is here and she's not happy.'

Emma gulped. 'What's wrong with her?'

'She won't say. She wants to see you.'

And this is where my career comes tumbling down. 'I'll be there in twenty minutes.'

'Great. I'll let her know.'

Emma disconnected the call. 'Right, I'm off to work. I'll see you later.'

Hope shrugged. 'All right. Catch you later.'

Instead of walking, Emma caught the next bus to Lambeth. Her mind was racing. Something had been niggling at the back of her mind since they'd left the florist, but she couldn't put her finger on it. She had wanted to talk it through with Lauren, but that would have to wait.

She thought back to that morning's events: Mike and his 'don't give a damn' attitude, the black rose, the florist claiming Lauren had sent the flower to herself, and Hope's belief that Lauren was playing some kind of sick game. Despite what it looked like, Emma believed Lauren was telling the truth.

The bus came to a halt at her stop and she hopped

off. Only a week or so had passed since Lauren had unexpectedly reappeared in her life, but it might as well have been a lifetime ago. So much had happened to her since then, and for the first time in her adult life, she felt like a whole person. *And it's all because of Lauren.*

Walking up the steps to her office building, she caught sight of Gina talking to a thin, blonde woman by the entrance. She recognised her as Louise's mum. They were the spitting image of each other.

'Here she is,' Gina said, one arm outstretched toward Emma.

And this is where I get fired!

'Will you both come into my office, please?'

They filed into the building and down the corridor to Gina's office.

'Please, sit down.' Gina gestured to the two empty seats opposite her desk.

As they lowered themselves into the chairs, Emma turned to Louise's mum. *Might as well get it over with. Why prolong the agony?* 'If this is about me showing up at your—'

Louise's mum shook her head. 'I'm not here because you showed up on our doorstep despite us asking you not to.'

Emma looked at Gina. 'You're not?'

Mrs Willis clasped her hands together. 'No. I'm here because I'm at a loss for what to do. Louise won't leave her room unless she absolutely needs to. She's barely eaten a thing since … since … well, you know what happened.'

'Has Louise spoken to you about that night?'

'She hasn't said a word, not that I can blame her. I'm ashamed that we didn't exactly deal with it in an appropriate manner, but we'd like to move forward.'

'Move forward?' Emma asked no one in particular. If Louise hadn't told her parents about Jay, she wouldn't either, so how could they make any progress? Emma didn't understand why Gina had called her into this meeting.

'What Mrs Willis means, Emma, is that she would like you to talk to Louise again. See if you can get her to engage.'

'Let her guard down,' Mrs Willis added.

'That's if she wants to speak to me again,' Emma said.

'Of course she does. You're the only person she will speak to.'

'Okay, if you think it will work, I'll give it a go. When do you want me to see her?'

'Now. She's in the car,' Mrs Willis said rising to her feet.

'Sure. Just send her to my office.'

After Mrs Willis had left the room, Gina said to her quietly, 'Don't think you're off the hook. You went against my direct orders.'

'I know. But all's well that ends well, right?' she said hopefully.

A smile crept over Gina's face. 'I must say I've never agreed with the notion of pushing someone away from the person they love in order to keep them close. It defeats the objective, doesn't it?'

A fleeting thought crossed Emma's mind. Hope used to moan about Lauren's popularity and how she made her feel inadequate. Emma now remembered a time when Hope had said something about how great it would be if Lauren just disappeared. Emma gripped the sides of her chair.

No, it couldn't be. Hope's words replayed in her mind: *None of this would have happened if you had left her alone like I said.* She wanted to be wrong, but deep inside she knew it was a possibility. The only person who was connected to Lauren's past besides Mike was Hope.

***

Emma dialled Lauren's number again and heard the same message: 'The number you are calling is unavailable.'

Why did Lauren turn her phone off? Did I do something to upset her? Emma was the first to admit she had been nonplussed by the drama at the florist. The florist's accusation had been hard to get her head around. Why would a complete stranger lie about such a thing, and straight to Lauren's face? It was mind boggling. But she wouldn't disclose those thoughts to Lauren in a million years. Footsteps neared her office and she switched her phone off. She would try again later. Right now, Louise needed her.

'Come in, Louise,' Emma said and gestured for her to sit down. Her face was gaunt and pale. Emma nearly recoiled at the extreme change in the young woman.

Louise dragged her feet as she entered the office and looked at Emma testily, as if waiting for Emma to have a go at her.

'It's all right.' Emma gave her a reassuring smile. 'Come on, sit down.'

'I'm sorry, Ms Clary,' Louise said, then broke down, sobbing.

Emma was out of her seat and beside Louise in seconds. This was the last thing she'd wanted—for Louise to feel like her help was conditional. Bar murder or anything illegal, she would always be committed to helping Louise through any hardship.

'Are you angry with me?'

'Of course not,' Emma said, trying to sound upbeat. 'You've done nothing wrong.'

'Not even when I refused to stick up for Jay?'

'Jay? Not at all. Do you want to talk about him?'

'You do realise, he's, you know—'

'Pre-op? Yes, I realise. What I don't understand is why you didn't tell me about him. I thought that was the point of coming to see me.'

'I didn't tell you about him because he wasn't important. Not at the time, anyway.'

Emma had to tread gently. She didn't want Louise to clam up. But if she was going to have any chance at helping her, she needed to know where Louise was at mentally.

'He seems very much in love with you. Do you know that?' Emma asked. 'He thinks he has a future with you. Is that how you feel too?'

'Yes. I want a future with him as well, but it's not that easy. I have to consider my mum and dad.'

'Your parents aren't the ones in a relationship with Jay.'

'No, but—'

'You can't live your life trying to please others.'

Louise's eyes brimmed with tears. 'I know, but they just about accepted me being a lesbian. I'd hate to imagine what they'd say if they found out Jay was transgender. It would be too far out of their comfort zone. I don't want to lose everyone because of him. I don't think any amount of love can make up for losing your entire family and friends, can it?'

'When you love someone, Louise, you'll move heaven and earth to be with them. No matter what. Take it from me. I know.'

Chapter Twenty-Nine

Lauren walked into her tastefully decorated attic apartment, went straight to the window, and drew the curtains back. In the distance, she could see the top part of the Eiffel Tower. No matter how much she loved Paris and her cosy little retreat, it was not her real home. Not really. London was. She squeezed her eyes shut and tried to drown out the thought that two hundred miles away, in London, was where her heart was.

Returning to Paris had been the most sensible thing to do. *Cowardly thing, you mean.*

She should have known she wasn't strong enough to face the monster that had been shadowing her most of her life—even with Emma by her side.

Frankie had agreed it was better for her to go home then return to London on the day of the exhibition. She could tell by the shakiness in his voice that he feared she wouldn't turn up at all. He should know better. Letting people down wasn't something she made a habit of, unless it was absolutely necessary.

Moving away from the window, Lauren ran her fingertip along the row of books on the shelf, looking for one she hadn't read to get her through what would be a long night. She picked out one by James Patterson, that's just what she needed—a fast paced thriller to keep her mind occupied.

Retrieving her phone from her pocket, she switched

it on. Several messages begged for her attention. Ignoring Fiona's texts, she clicked open Emma's. They were frantic. She was desperate to know where she was. Guilt stabbed at her heart. She'd been selfish, running away without a second thought about how Emma would feel. But fear was hard to turn down.

She dialled her number and Emma answered the call on the first ring.

'Lauren, where are you? I've been trying to get in touch with you since yesterday.'

'I—'

'It doesn't matter. Where are you now? We need to talk.'

'I'm in Paris,' Lauren said.

She heard Emma's quick intake of breath. 'Paris! What are you doing there?'

'I came back because …' Words escaped her. *Because you think I made the stalker up and I'm lying. I don't feel safe, even with you.*

Despite the truth of those thoughts, she couldn't reveal them to Emma. She would no doubt deny it anyway, and as much as Lauren wanted to believe in her, she couldn't. Lauren knew what she'd heard, including the doubt in Emma's voice.

Through the momentary silence, Lauren could sense Emma's desperation urging her to continue.

'Because it was the right thing to do. I can't take it anymore, Emma.'

'I think we've been looking at the wrong person.'

Lauren conjured up an image of Emma pacing the

floor of her apartment, pushing together puzzle pieces that would never fit no matter how hard she forced them. 'Emma, you have to let this go. The police can't do anything about Mike, and he's too clever to slip up.'

'That's because he isn't your stalker. I think it's Hope.'

'Hope! Why didn't I see this coming? So it's gone from Mike'—*to me stalking myself*—'to Hope. Who's next? Your stepdad?'

Emma's tone was serious when she said, 'Just hear me out. The day I got my binoculars, Hope came around, and we were—' She paused. 'We were looking around for a bit. Hope had the binoculars trained on your building, having a nosey. She seemed into it, but then, for no reason, she decided she wanted to go inside.'

'I'm not following. So she lost interest. How does that make her a stalker?'

'That in itself doesn't, but she must have seen you in your apartment. I didn't put the two together until I realised your apartment was burgled the very next day.'

'Are … are you saying you think it was Hope from the beginning?'

'That's exactly what I'm saying. She was around when it happened at school, and it's a bit of a coincidence that it started up again when you came back to London.'

Lauren felt for the sofa behind her and sank into it. She had been friendly with Hope at school. A bad word had never been spoken between them. Lauren had always been kind to her.

'But why would she do that? What reason would she have to ruin my life?'

'I don't know.'

'I can't believe it.'

'I didn't want to either, but it's the only explanation I can come up with.'

'But what's her motive?'

'From the research I did on stalkers, it seems like they don't need one,' Emma ranted. 'I wish we hadn't told Hope we were fitting the peephole with a security camera. If we hadn't given her a heads-up on what we were doing, we could have caught her in the act.'

Lauren chose her words carefully. She didn't want to make a commitment on something she couldn't follow through with. 'Do you think I should come back to confront her?'

'No, that's the last thing you should do. As much as I miss you after only a day apart, I can't bear to see how this whole thing is affecting you. If anything, I'll come and see you in Paris.'

'I wish you could come tonight,' Lauren said, forgetting her feelings of betrayal. The situation was so messed up it was hard to know what to believe.

'Don't tempt me. The sooner we sort this mess out, the quicker you can get on with making a fresh start.'

'What if Hope denies it all?'

'It doesn't matter. The fact we're on to her will be enough. I could kill her. I really could when I think of the misery she put you and your family through. I'm going round to see her. Let's see what she has to say for herself, shall we?'

'I should have stayed and faced up to things from the start. I shouldn't have run away like a coward.'

'You were sixteen, barely an adult. How were you supposed to know how to deal with this? Even celebrities have a hard time shaking them loose, and they've got money and power.'

'I wish you were here.'

'Me too.'

'Do you want to Skype me when you get in bed, and we can fall asleep together?'

'I'd like nothing better. Speak later then. I …'

'I know, Emma. Me too.'

Lauren disconnected the call and held the phone against her chest, closing her eyes. If Hope was responsible for causing her to flee and make a new life, she didn't know if she could face her again. It was a tough call, especially since Hope was Emma's stepsister and Lauren knew how fiercely Emma protected those she loved. If it was Hope, she would have to follow Emma's lead. She could never ask her to choose her over her sister.

She wondered again if this was the end to her problem. If, as Emma had predicted, Hope stopped harassing her once she caught wind they were on to her, Lauren would at last find some sort of balance in her life.

Chapter Thirty

Emma stood in front of Hope's house. Until that very moment, she hadn't realised how much she didn't want to go in. Confrontation wasn't her strong suit, and what she was planning on asking Hope wasn't nice—especially if she was wrong.

The front door creaked open and Hope emerged. 'Hi, Emma. To what do I owe the pleasure?' she said, beckoning her in.

'I was just on my way home from work and thought I'd pop by,' Emma said, stepping over the threshold.

'Come into the kitchen. I'm making vegetable soup. Beer?' Hope overtook her in the long hallway and veered left into the large, spacious kitchen.

The thought of sharing a beer with someone who had mentally tortured Lauren made her physically ill. *Just act like you would on any other night.*

'I'd love one, thanks.'

'So, where's Lauren?' Hope asked, taking two beers from the fridge and flipping their lids off with a bottle opener. She handed one to Emma and placed her own next to the chopping board where she resumed chopping a carrot.

'Busy. She's got some guys round her place.' Emma was careful not to meet Hope's gaze and instead fiddled with the bottle's label. Hope was a human lie detector; she could catch Emma in a lie in a split second.

It's a pity I can't say the same.

'Guys?' Hope raised her brows.

Emma cleared her throat, hoping she could pull this off. 'Yeah, something to do with lifting fingerprints off the letter she received the other day.'

'I thought only the police could do that sort of thing?' Hope threw the carrots into a stainless steel colander and moved to rinse them under the sink. She grabbed a bunch of celery from the side and handed it to Emma. 'Here, you can cut these.'

Emma took the celery from her. 'You know, businesses on the internet. You can find a company for just about anything these days. Just think, you can have your genetic code mapped out just by providing a swab. Taking someone's fingerprint should be a doddle.'

Emma waited until Hope moved away from the sink and washed her hands. She removed a knife from the drawer, put several celery stalks on a plate, and started chopping.

'Lauren's more than convinced it isn't Mike stalking her now. She thinks it's someone else. Someone with a grudge.'

Hope emptied the carrots into a large pot of water on the hob and stirred them with a wooden spoon. 'Why doesn't that surprise me? Believe me, the only prints they'll find are hers.'

Yeah, because you probably wore gloves. Emma kept her tone light as she said, 'Or the nutty stalker's.'

Hope stared back at her, big blue eyes flashing with disdain. 'I wish you'd stop using that word.'

'Why, that's what they are. Creepy little fuckers who don't have a life and feed on the fear of others. At the same time, they don't have the guts to make themselves known. They have to inflict their pain from the shadows like the cowards they are.'

'Whoa, that's a bit harsh,' Hope said, grabbing the plate with the celery on it. Several pieces fell over the edge and onto the floor. Hope grunted and swooped down to pick them up. She rinsed them off and threw them into the pot.

Emma wondered if Hope was getting riled up because she wasn't buying her story of Lauren stalking herself. Whatever the reason, she decided to keep pushing to see where it led. 'Is it? What would you call them?'

'I don't know. Whoever it is might be crying out for help.'

'In which case they should see a psychiatrist.' It was taking all of Emma's strength not to put her hands around Hope's neck and strangle the life out of her. 'Anyway, it's not important. Technology today isn't like it was fourteen years ago. If the scumbag goes anywhere near her apartment again, we'll find out who it is once and for all.'

'Then you and Lauren will live happily ever after, I take it.'

'Who knows?'

Hope spun round and stared at Emma challengingly. 'Come on. You know that's what you want. You've been pining over her since she left school.'

Emma studied her closely. Was this what it was all about? 'You sound like you have a problem with that.'

'Oh please. Why would I. And I'm also not the one who thinks the sun shines out of her rear.'

'Jealousy, envy—who knows. I always got the impression you didn't like her, and I could never figure out why, until now.'

Faint puzzlement lingered on Hope's face. 'What are you talking about?'

'You're jealous of her, aren't you? And you were back at school,' Emma said, remembering the snide comments Hope had made when Emma would rave about Lauren from afar.

Without blinking or hesitating, Hope said, 'Yeah, of course I was. It's not like I ever denied it. She's beautiful, talented, and can have anyone she wants. What isn't there to be jealous of?'

'Jealous enough to make her want to disappear?' Emma dried her hands on a tea towel and moved towards her.

Hope raised her hand, stopping Emma in her tracks. 'Where exactly are we going with this?'

'You can stop lying, Hope.'

Hope picked up the knife she had been using to cut the carrot, her fierce expression like a neon warning sign. For an instant, Emma had the ridiculous notion that Hope would attack her. A surge of relief rushed through her when Hope reached for a loose onion on the counter.

'Hold on a minute. Do you think I'm behind all of

this?'

An awkward silence fell between them as Emma regained her composure. The front door was only a few feet away if things turned ugly, but she had to keep pushing. She needed to know the truth. 'Aren't you? You just admitted you were jealous of her.'

'Yes, jealous, like most girls were. But not enough to want to drive her insane. How can you think that of me?'

Emma backed against the wall as Hope came at her. She flinched when Hope snatched the bottle of beer from her, using the hand holding the knife. 'Why don't you fuck off back to her? It's obvious you prefer her company to mine.'

She was glad Hope's intention wasn't to stab her, but still feeling uncomfortable, Emma edged her way to the kitchen door. 'It's not even remotely the same, Hope. I'm in love with her.'

'No, you're infatuated with an imaginary person you built up in your head. You're forgetting how she left you behind while she went on to make a new life for herself. And believe me, she'll drop you again as soon as it suits her. That's who she is, and the sooner you get your head out of the clouds, the sooner you'll see I'm right.'

'You're wrong.'

'We'll see. The only person Lauren cares about is Lauren. You'll find out soon enough, and then there'll be no hiding from it.'

Emma stumbled through the doorway, Hope's

words hitting her like a punch in the gut. Was she right? After all, Lauren had picked up and left without telling her. If they did get back together by some miracle, would Lauren run away at the first sign of trouble? The thought frightened her. *Am I setting myself up for another fall?*

Chapter Thirty-One

At eleven o'clock, Lauren sat in bed, her laptop open in front of her, and the Skype window ready for when Emma called. She had thought about wearing something revealing, but realised she didn't actually own anything that would pass as such. Instead she wore a grey vest and polka dot pyjama bottoms. *Sexy.*

Why hadn't Emma contacted her yet? Lauren thought that was the first thing she would do after confronting Hope. Emma finished work at five and would have gone straight round there. It was now 9pm.

Did Hope hurt Emma during her confrontation? Lauren doubted it. She couldn't imagine a woman of Hope's petite size doing much damage to Emma, who was taller and stronger than her. *Then why hasn't she called?*

Her anxiety level rising, she slipped out of bed and went to the kitchen to make chamomile tea. The drink normally soothed her nerves. After pouring hot water over the teabag, she picked up the mug and made her way back to her bedroom. Twenty minutes later, with the contents of her cup gone, Lauren was still waiting for Emma to call.

Impatience got the better of Lauren so she grabbed her mobile from the bedside table and called her. After two rings the line went to voicemail. She waited a few seconds before trying again. This time her call went straight to voicemail. Assuming that Emma's battery was flat, she waited half an hour before calling once more.

By one in the morning and with no luck getting through, fatigue enveloped Lauren and she closed the laptop. She snuggled under the covers and decided not to panic yet. She'd call Emma in the morning.

***

The sound of early morning traffic outside her window filtered into Lauren's subconscious. She stretched out her arm and caressed the space beside her, still caught up in her dream of Emma. It took her brain a few seconds to realise she was in bed alone, and her eyes flashed opened. Sadness tore at her heart as she took in the empty space where Emma should have been. The thought of never again waking up with Emma by her side made her want to weep.

Finding her phone amongst the ruffled bedclothes, she sank her head back against the pillow and checked for any new messages. Nothing. She dialled Emma's number, and relief shot through her when it rang. For the next few seconds, the call went unanswered, then her voicemail picked up. This time she left a message.

'Emma, it's me. I'm getting really worried. Can you call me back ASAP? Otherwise I'll think something's happened to you.' She paused, fidgeting with the edge of the quilt. 'I missed talking to you last night,' she said and ended the call.

She headed into the bathroom and brushed her teeth. Just as she was about to turn the shower on, her mobile phone rang. Hurrying back to her bedroom, she prayed it was Emma. Seeing her name flash up, she grinned and flopped down on the bed.

'Where've you been? I thought you were going to call me last night.'

'Something came up.' Emma sounded cold and distant.

'Is everything all right? You sound funny.'

'Everything's fine.'

'Oh, okay,' Lauren said, more convinced that something was amiss. The joviality and chattiness she had become accustomed to were definitely missing. 'How are things at work?'

'Busy.'

'Okay, enough of this. If you're pissed off with me, just spit it out.'

'I'm not pissed off with you,' Emma said coolly.

'Has Hope been saying things about me?'

'Only the truth.'

'Which is?'

Emma sounded reluctant as she said, 'That I don't really know you. That I'm seeing you as I want to see you rather than the reality.'

Lauren snorted. 'Now I've heard it all. Who exactly am I meant to be?'

'I don't know. That's the problem. It seems to be a pattern with you. You come into my life, make me feel amazing, then you disappear.'

'You know why I left.'

'I know, but Hope's right. You'll always leave

when things don't turn out right.'

'Is that what you really believe?'

'Can you prove otherwise?

Lauren racked her brain to come up with a suitable answer.

'Exactly,' Emma said, breaking the long silence. 'Look, I've got to go.'

'Emma, please don't leave things like this. Let's Skype so we can at least see each other while we're talking.'

'Apart from telling you I was wrong about Hope, I have nothing else to say.'

'Emma—'

The line went dead.

So Hope's done a right number on me. She wouldn't have minded, but she wasn't even there to defend herself against these accusations. *As if I'm the sort of person who runs away.* She looked at herself in the mirror. *You can lie to others, Lauren, but don't lie to yourself.*

Hope was right. Lauren was a quitter, and everyone knew it except her. There was only one way to prove to Emma she would always be with her, no matter the obstacles Lauren faced in her life. She would have to face her biggest fear and return to London.

Chapter Thirty-Two

Emma brushed away the single tear running down her cheek. She wouldn't cry. There wasn't any point. She would have been prolonging her agony if she hadn't ended their 'relationship'. Lauren had literally confirmed what Hope had said about her—that she would always be on the run. With little chance of finding out who was stalking her, what future did they have? Her feelings for Lauren ran deep enough that she didn't want her to come back to London if she was in danger. As much as it hurt, things were better this way, though it meant letting go of the dream she'd nearly had in her grasp.

Jack walked past her open door then doubled back, his face full of concern. 'Hey, are you all right?'

'Great. Never better,' she said, messing with her hair.

'Come on, talk to Uncle Jack,' he said, dropping into the seat opposite her. 'Has Wendy been on your case again?'

'I wish it were something that simple.'

'I'm listening.'

'It's everything. People who I thought were decent turned out not to be. A woman who I thought cared about me doesn't. My mum keeps putting her husband before me. Need I go on?'

'That's some baggage you've got there.'

'Tell me about it.'

'You know what the solution is, don't you?'

'No, what?'

He grinned sheepishly. 'Shit, I thought you were going to tell me, because I have no idea.'

'At least you're honest.'

'Yeah, there is that. Seriously though, you can't do anything about your mum and your lady. There comes a point when you have to realise you won't always see eye to eye with people, especially those closest to you. You might see the big picture from the outside, but that's you. You can't be a hero to everyone, no matter how much you want to be.'

He rose to his feet and left the room.

Emma bowed her head. She didn't want to be a hero; she wanted to help people, but how? By taking their power away to make their own decisions? That didn't sound helpful in the least. She thought about how she'd disobeyed Gina's request to give Louise space. *I thought I knew best.*

Then she considered her attempts to make Lauren stay despite how vulnerable and scared she felt, because she thought she could charge in and save the day by finding her stalker—and failing miserably in the process. *Colombo, I'm not.*

Then off she went on her high horse, accusing innocent people of stalking Lauren without having a shred of evidence. *Again, because I thought I knew better.*

When it came to her mother, though, she couldn't see for the life of her what she had done to create the distance between them. She shouldn't have to make an appointment to see her mother as if she were a stranger. *Maybe I have to accept that she no longer wants the close mother/daughter relationship we once shared and that's her prerogative.*

Jack was right. She had to let people walk their own paths without interfering. It wasn't as if she had made anything better for anyone.

Emma couldn't help Lauren now that she'd returned to Paris, but it wasn't too late for her to make amends with Louise.

***

'Thanks for coming in,' Emma said awkwardly.

'You said it was important.' Louise sat across from her.

'It is. I want to apologise. I was in the wrong. I shouldn't have badgered you the way I did.'

Louise shifted in her seat and stared down at her hands. 'So you're saying I shouldn't say anything to my parents about Jay?'

'What I'm saying is you should only tell them if it's what you think is best.'

'I already decided it's best they know the truth. I don't want Jay to have a black mark against his name with them thinking he hurt me. And you were right. If you love someone, nothing should stand in the way.'

Emma stopped herself from reacting and thought about her response. 'And what will you do if your parents reject him?'

'Then they'll miss out on knowing an amazing person.' Louise stopped. When she spoke again, her voice had the effect of energising the room. 'We're moving to Reading in a couple of weeks. Jay's uncle offered him a job at his computer firm, and I'm going to college. We want to make a fresh start for ourselves where no one knows me.'

'I'm happy for you, Louise. I really am.'

'Do you think I'm making the right choice?'

Let her walk her own path. 'I think you know yourself best. Trust your gut instinct and follow it, no matter what anyone else says. Me included.'

Chapter Thirty-Three

Thanks to half a bottle of Merlot on the Eurostar, Lauren arrived back in London less anxious than she would have been sober—though that didn't stop her from getting a taxi to Emma's apartment. *No point in tempting fate.*

Lauren had been preparing what she wanted to say to Emma, but she was still uncertain whether Emma would actually believe her.

The taxi dropped her outside the apartment block, and Lauren trudged her suitcase behind her up to the intercom. She buzzed and waited. No reply. She pressed her finger to the buzzer again. Nothing. Noting it was after six on her phone, Lauren presumed Emma had been caught up at work. She decided she would wait until a resident entered or left to get inside the building and go up under her own steam. Leaning against the wall, she thought how funny it was that alcohol could mask a person's basic fear. Here she was out in the open, and all she felt was excitement about seeing Emma. Whether she'd feel that way when she was sober was another matter.

Lauren's heart stuttered when she recognised Emma's familiar gait crossing the street. As Emma neared, Lauren saw her eyes widen and her lips part. Whether her surprise was a good sign, she couldn't tell.

'I thought you were in Paris,' Emma said, inserting

her key into the lock and pushing the door open.

'I was. We need to talk,' Lauren said, trailing behind her to the lift.

'I told you I don't have anything to say.'

'Well I do.'

The doors to the lift opened and Emma stepped inside.

Heart pounding, Lauren had no time to think. If those doors closed, she could kiss goodbye any chance of making amends. Once Emma was inside her apartment, it would be even harder to get to her.

She took a deep breath and jumped into the lift just before the doors shut.

'Lauren, what are you doing?' Emma asked, frantically hitting the button to open the doors, having already pressed the button for her floor.

It was too late. The lift was ascending.

'Oh my God, I don't know.' Lauren closed her eyes as her heart plummeted into her stomach.

Focus, breathe, focus, breathe. She willed the lift not to stop. *This was such a bad idea.*

Emma wrapped her arms around her. 'It's okay. There's just two more floors to go. You're doing great.'

Lauren gripped her arm and gave her a small nod of gratitude.

'One more to go and we're there,' Emma said.

The lift stopped and panic filled every cell of her body.

Emma held her tighter. 'It takes a few seconds for the doors to open. Don't worry.'

The doors slid open, and so did Lauren's eyes. She broke away from Emma and leapt out of the lift before bending over and inhaling deeply. Emma was by her side, gently rubbing her back.

'Come on, let's go to my apartment. It was silly getting into the lift if it puts you in this kind of state,' Emma said as if talking to a child.

'I seem to be doing many silly things lately,' Lauren admitted. *Like leaving instead of telling you I heard your conversation with Hope.* She had come to realise it was reasonable to have doubts, especially if someone you trusted—like Hope, in Emma's case—threw a new light on things. Perhaps Hope really did believe Lauren was unstable and she was only looking out for Emma. For that she couldn't blame her.

Once inside, Lauren dropped onto Emma's sofa, her initial panic from being in the lift dissolving. It didn't matter how many times she tried to convince herself claustrophobia was an irrational fear; the advice never quite sunk in. Maybe it was because deep down she didn't believe it. *What's irrational about not wanting to be trapped in a metal coffin?* No, she'd stick to taking the stairs over a lift any day.

'I'll get you a glass of water,' Emma said kindly.

'Thanks,' Lauren muttered.

Emma returned and handed a glass to Lauren. She perched on the edge of the coffee table, resting her elbows on her legs.

'Why did you come back?' she asked matter-of-factly.

Lauren grimaced and placed the glass on the table next to Emma.

'Because I missed you so much and I'm willing to go through anything if it means being with you.' She gently stroked Emma's cheek, her soft skin like silk against her fingers.

Emma's eyes widened and her breath hitched. She didn't back away, which told Lauren she'd made the right choice in touching her.

'For how long?' Emma murmured. She pressed her hand over Lauren's, and the warmth of her palm sent waves of longing through her.

'I only left because I overheard you speaking to Hope. I was hurt. I thought you didn't believe me.'

'Lauren, I never said I doubted you. I never have. Not for one minute.'

'I know, but Hope did. I guess I'd just had enough.'

'And therein lies the problem. What about the next time you've "had enough"? I don't know if I can trust you and let my guard down with you without worrying every time we face an obstacle. I don't want to live my life walking on egg shells.'

Lauren let the words float around in her mind. If she was going to commit to Emma, she had to be sure—for both their sakes. A feeling of certainty filled her upon seeing Emma's gaze. The look of love and tenderness told her everything she needed to know. Lauren was going forward with her life from now on. There would be no U-turns. Not ever again. Not when it came to Emma.

'You won't have to. Let me prove myself to you. I won't leave you again, Emma. I promise.'

'Even if—'

A little grin twisted Lauren's lips. 'Even if I have a million and one stalkers hunting me down.'

'If you had that many, I'd go into hiding myself,' Emma joked.

'Let's hope it never comes to that.'

'Speaking of stalkers—'

'Oh God, I forgot to ask you about your encounter with Hope.' She inwardly cringed as she imagined the confrontation. 'I take it she wasn't too thrilled to have you accuse her of being my stalker.'

Emma's expression turned from neutral to one of sadness. 'That's an understatement. She took it pretty badly. Not that I blame her.'

'So you definitely don't think it's her?'

'No. I think her beef with you is just female competitiveness,' Emma said heavily. 'For some reason, she thinks you're a threat to our friendship. Which leads us back to Mike again.'

Lauren hated the thought of them falling out over her. 'Me? I would never come between—'

'There's no need to tell me that. I know you wouldn't. But it's not me who needs convincing. It's Hope. Seeing as I don't think she'll ever talk to me again, convincing her might be difficult.'

'Give it some time. She'll understand once she's calmed down.'

'You do know we're talking about Hope here?'

Emma said.

'Yes, and that's why I know she'll forgive and forget. She cares about you too much to hold a grudge.'

'I hope you're right. Listen, before I forget, I was thinking about something you said a few days ago—about the stereotypical stalker.'

'What, him looking like a crazy person?'

'No. The part about him having pictures of you in his room. I have an idea but it's totally up to you. I don't want to pressure you into anything. Especially after the mess I've made of everything so far.'

'Go on, I'm listening.'

'If we could somehow get into Mike's place ...'

Lauren didn't object, but she did need clarification. 'Are you talking about breaking-in?'

'I remember reading on his Facebook page that he lives in a flat share with two other geeks—his choice of words, not mine. How do you think they'll react if two very sexy school friends of Mike's turn up unannounced and ask to wait for him until he gets home from work?'

'But he unfriended you.'

'Yes, me, but I noticed he's also friends with Jillian who we went to school with. I've spoken to her a couple of times on messenger, I'm sure she won't mind giving me the info we need.'

'So when shall we go?' If truth be told, Lauren wasn't up for any drama that night, she just wanted to stay at home with Emma and relax.

'I'll have to check when he's working. Not tonight though, I thought we'd make up for lost time first. It has been two whole days,' Emma said, unbuttoning Lauren's shirt.

'You won't hear any complaints from me,' Lauren said, letting her shirt fall to her waist.

'You are so beautiful.' Emma brushed Lauren's hair from her face and kissed her softly. 'I've loved you for so long. I don't know what it's like to not love you.'

Lauren opened her mouth to tell Emma she felt the same, but Emma pressed her finger against her lips.

'Before, what I felt for you was like a dream. This'—Emma pulled down Lauren's bra straps, tugging until Lauren's breasts slipped free from their confines—'is more than I ever thought I could have.'

Emma cupped Lauren's breasts in her hands and rolled her nipples between her fingers. Lauren moaned and leant into Emma's touch.

'I worry that even though I love you, it won't be enough, and I don't think I could stand losing you,' Emma said.

Understanding finally filtered through Lauren's mind and the pieces fell into place. 'I promise I'll never leave you.'

Lauren turned Emma around and laid her on the sofa. Red cushions served as a colourful backsplash to Emma's body as she teasingly removed her clothes, laying her naked before her. She kissed her sweet lips while her hand trailed down Emma's sensitive skin, all the way to her core. There, her fingers touched Emma, tautening her body with each caress. Lauren kissed her neck and her shoulder and suckled at her breasts, whispering as she went, 'You're more than I ever deserved. Before you, I only existed. With you, I know what living is.'

Emma cried out, her skin trembling as Lauren brought her over the edge. Panting, Emma looked up at Lauren, her eyes hot and darker than their usual light brown.

Without warning, Emma turned her over. Lauren found herself on her back, Emma straddling her hips.

Grabbing Lauren's wrists, Emma held them over Lauren's head.

'You drive me crazy,' Emma whispered as she rubbed herself on Lauren, her breasts teasing her mouth.

Lauren melted, losing herself in Emma's touch and the feel of her skin, her heat. Emma's nimble tongue circled her nipple. She let go of Lauren's wrists and her hand drifted down between her thighs, her fingers playing with Lauren's centre. Pleasure exploded within as she lightly stroked her.

Lauren almost came apart. 'I love you.'

Grabbing Emma's face, Lauren brought her lips to hers, submerging herself in her taste, with love and worry mingling there.

'I'm so happy you came back,' Emma said and pulled away to look at Lauren.

Tears welled in Lauren's eyes and she nodded. Then she pushed Emma's hands away and reclaimed her mouth.

No more words. They would speak with their bodies, letting the language of their skin relay their words for them.

Lauren's hands roamed everywhere—on the elegant arch of Emma's spine and that little spot on the back of her shoulder blades that drove Emma wild when Lauren caressed it a certain way.

Emma groaned and arched, Lauren forcing her fingers deep into Emma. They whimpered from the extra contact. Emma held herself up, her hands bracketed on either side of Lauren. The angle allowed Lauren full access to Emma's breasts, and while Emma rocked against her feverish touch, Lauren took her nipple into her mouth, savouring it, letting Emma's shivers and sighs drive her further.

Love bloomed as they paid homage to each other. Unspoken declarations infused the space around them, creating a sanctuary where they were the only ones.

Sweat slicked their skin. They grew hotter and more desperate with each teasing touch, desire rushing inside them, fueling them as they drove each other harder and faster.

They held on to each other as they flew over the edge of ecstasy. Again and again.

Chapter Thirty-Four

The mixture of their perfumes in the car was overwhelming. Emma lowered the window to inhale a lungful of air. She glanced sideways at Lauren's profile. She looked serious, as if they were getting ready to rob a bank and she was considering everything that could go wrong. Emma pretty much felt the same—until her gaze dropped to Lauren's naked leg, exposed from the short black skirt she wore.

To think it was only last night I was running my tongue along them. Her insides tingled with desire at the thought. Her phone pinged with a Facebook message. Jillian had messaged her, letting her know Mike was at his job in Lewisham, although she wasn't sure how long he had been there. Emma thanked her and put her phone into her bag.

'Are you ready to get this over with?' Emma asked.

'Are you?'

Emma pressed her palm against her chest as if she could somehow slow her pounding heart. She cursed herself for her stupid idea of playing cop with Lauren. She had no idea how things would pan out, but she hoped, for their sakes, that Mike's roommates were geeks like Mike, and not the size of rugby players.

'Yes, let's do it.'

They exited the car and held on to the side of the vehicle as they acclimatised to their six-inch heels.

Emma's blood flow to her pinched toes ceased. She had never worn anything so high in her life.

Dragging their feet, they crossed the road and headed toward the imposing Victorian house. Emma checked her phone. Jillian was their look out and would message Emma if Mike left for home.

Holding on to the wooden rail for support, Emma went up the stairs first. They'd agreed that Emma would do the talking and keep their attention, while Lauren excused herself to the bathroom and located Mike's room.

Emma took a deep breath, then knocked.

The door flew open, and Emma could have kissed the floor. A thin, bespectacled man stood at the entrance with a gaming console handset in his hand. When he saw them, his mouth dropped open.

Finding his voice, he asked, 'Are you lost or something?'

Emma gave him a slow, seductive smile. 'Not if this is where Mike lives.'

His eyes widened. 'Mike? You know Mike?'

'Uh-huh. We went to school together.'

His eyes darted between them. 'Well, that figures. He's not in.'

'I know. We just got into town from …'

'Brighton,' Lauren said, filling in for her.

'Yeah, Brighton,' she said, regaining her composure. 'He said he was working at Tesco tonight, but he'd party with us after.'

'Mike, party? Are you sure you've got the right guy?'

'If you knew him like we did.' Lauren winked.

'Wow, really? The dark horse.' He chuckled.

'Would you mind if we waited for him to get back from work. I know we're early but we've had a long drive.'

'Sure.' He stepped back to let them into the large foyer: white walls, dark blue carpet, and a mountain bike resting against a wall with a pile of winter coats strewn atop it. A faint, musky odour permeated the area, but nothing too hideous.

'Come and wait in the living room. Do you want a drink? He'll be a while.'

'Sure. You got any beer?'

'Sure do.' He smirked.

'Do you mind if I use your loo? I'm bursting,' Emma asked.

Mike's flatmate ignored her request. His eyes remained glued on Lauren's shapely legs.

'Where's the toilet?' Lauren asked.

'The toilet? Um, upstairs, first door on the left.'

Lauren looked at him suggestively while trailing a finger down his chest. 'Next to your room?'

His face reddened. 'No, mine is opposite.'

Bingo! One down, two to check.

'So what beer you got?' Emma heard Lauren ask as she took the stairs.

Reaching the landing, she scanned the layout. Five doors in total. She pushed the first one to the left. *Right, that's the bathroom.*

Emma looked at the door opposite. *That's his room.*

She walked farther along the narrow hall and opened the door on the right. The room was immaculate, with blue curtains and matching bedding. Trainer boxes were lined up in a neat row against the wall under the window. It didn't strike her as the sort of room Mike would live in. Despite this, she slipped out of her shoes and tiptoed to the TV stand, where several framed pictures were on display. One showed a young man with long, scraggly hair holding a guitar. Another picture showed the same man holding a puppy. Satisfied, she tiptoed to the room opposite.

Oh, this is definitely Mike's room. The place looked like a bomb had gone off. The bed was unmade. Clothes that seemed like they hadn't been washed for weeks were scattered everywhere. Plates and cups were on the floor by the side of the bed. If it wasn't for the open window, Emma was sure she would have gagged.

Dumbfounded, she stood there, unsure where to start. There was nothing in plain view that suggested Mike was Lauren's stalker. There wasn't anything sinister either. No pictures of Lauren's head superimposed on naked bodies, or her face on a dartboard with pinholes in it.

She crossed over to his wardrobe and pulled the door open to reveal more mayhem. Mike's idea of tidying up was to dump everything in the cupboard. *Out of sight, out of mind.*

Emma grimaced as she used the tips of her fingers to pull away some clothes lying on top of a box. Flipping the lid open, she moved the contents around. There wasn't much to see. She dug down to a thick folder at the bottom and pulled it out.

Her phone pinged. It was Jillian. Mike was on his way back. She didn't know how much time had passed since he'd left work, because, according to her message, Jillian had gone off to make dinner and it slipped her mind to keep checking.

Shit! Glancing down, she realised she was holding a photo album. Before she could flick through it, the front door slammed shut. She froze for several heartbeats, then dropped the folder back in the box, shut the cupboard door, and retraced her steps to the bathroom. She was in the middle of putting on her shoes when she heard raised voices, including Lauren's. With no time to think about who Lauren was shouting at or why, Emma scrambled downstairs and almost ran into Mike's back.

She staggered, but not from the sight of him. Lauren's eyes were wide and wild. She looked absolutely terrifying.

'Lauren, what is it?' Emma asked.

Mike didn't even bother to turn and face her. His eyes were fixed on Lauren.

'This,' Lauren said, holding up a photo.

Emma skirted around Mike to where Lauren was standing. Lauren thrust the picture into her hand. Emma first saw the writing on the back: *Mike & Claire Foster 2016*.

Puzzled, she turned it over, and it took a few seconds for her brain to process what she was actually seeing. The picture was of Mike at his thirtieth birthday bash. He was standing next to his sister—the florist they'd visited.

Chapter Thirty-Five

'I don't know what sick game you twisted fuckers are playing, but it stops now,' Lauren said.

Mike smoothed back his hair, looking well and truly busted.

'You're a stalker. Aren't you going to try and talk your way out of this one, Mike?' Emma asked.

'This isn't what you think. It really isn't,' Mike said.

Mike's flatmate, who was standing beside Lauren, said, 'Stalker! Shit, man, that's fucking sick. What's the matter with you?' When Mike didn't reply, his flatmate went on. 'Oh my God. I've had my kid sister stay here. I've got to call my mum.'

Lauren stared after him as he hurried away then she turned back to Mike. 'There's no getting out of it this time. I still have the flower you sent me. Your sister will have to tell the police the truth about who ordered it.'

Mike remained silent, enraging Lauren even more.

'You know what? Fuck you. I'll let the police deal with you.'

She brushed past him and glanced back to see that Emma was following her.

They'd reached the door when he finally spoke. 'Wait.'

Hand on the lock, Lauren looked back. 'Don't bother. Nothing you say will change anything.'

'Don't you want to hear the full story?'

'Does it really matter?'

Emma rested her hand on Lauren's forearm. 'Maybe you should hear him out. You might get some answers and finally be able to put all this behind you.'

'What can you possibly say that will make things any better?' Lauren asked Mike.

He stared at his trainers. 'I thought you were looking for the truth about why you were targeted.'

The air was sucked out of Lauren's lungs. She spun around, holding on to Emma for support. When she spoke, she couldn't stop her voice from shaking. 'Are you telling me you think you can actually justify putting me and my family through hell?'

'You really haven't put it together, have you?' he said.

Lauren didn't know whether he was apologizing or enjoying playing with her.

'Are you saying I did something to offend you?' she said sharply.

'Sit down and have a beer and I promise I'll tell you everything.'

Tamping down her frustration, Lauren said, 'You have ten minutes.'

'The short version won't even take five.'

They followed him into a cramped living space, which looked like a gaming room for kids. A massive wide-screen TV hung on the wall. Underneath it was a gaming console and stacks upon stacks of video games. Three single leather gaming chairs stood side by side, facing the screen.

Mike dropped into the middle seat and gestured for them to sit on either side. He was enjoying keeping her on tenterhooks.

'I'm not playing your sick game, Mike. Come on, Emma. Let's go.'

He leapt out of his seat and blocked her way.

'Look, I'm sorry. This isn't easy for me.'

'Isn't easy for you?' Lauren said. 'What the hell do you think it's been like for me?'

'Sorry. That came out wrong. What I mean is that it isn't easy to snitch on family.'

Lauren looked down at him. 'Snitch? What are you talking about?'

'It's my sister. She's the one who's been stalking you all this time.'

Chapter Thirty-Six

Standing at the counter in her kitchen, Emma poured Lauren a third glass of brandy, and like she had twice before, Lauren knocked it back in one go. Were she in Lauren's shoes, she would have needed something more than brandy to calm her nerves. The shock of the evening's events had left them reeling and struggling to make sense of Mike's bombshell. His sister, of all people, was responsible. Not an ex-partner or her jealous stepsister, but a near-enough stranger who Lauren barely had any contact with.

'I … I still can't believe it.'

Lauren was trembling, and Emma slid her arm around her waist to comfort her. 'Do you think he was telling the truth?'

'Why would he lie?'

'To cover his tracks.'

'No, I believe him. There's no reason to lie. Not now.'

'Come on. Let's take our drinks into the bedroom.'

Emma led Lauren along the hallway. 'I suppose I'd better text Hope and apologise.'

'I'd better ring my mum and dad. They're worried about me enough as it is.'

'Go and lie down. I'll get your phone.'

She walked into the kitchen and took Lauren's phone from her bag and collected her own. On the way back to the bedroom, she texted Hope and told her about the new development. She would wait to tell her face-to-face what an utter idiot she had been. Emma only hoped she could forgive her.

Lauren was sitting with her back against the headboard, holding an empty glass.

'You want another refill?'

'I think I've reached my limit.'

Emma handed Lauren her phone and stood by the window, looking out across the way while she sipped her brandy. She thought about how difficult it must be for Lauren, finding out that someone ruined her life because—well, they didn't actually know why. Mike had only realised it was his sister when Lauren showed him the letters and he recognised the handwriting. He'd kept them so Lauren wouldn't have any physical evidence against Claire. That was why the police's visit hadn't bothered him; he knew he was innocent, and they couldn't pin anything on him.

All Emma could do was be thankful it was truly over. Well, it would be once they visited Claire Foster and confirmed she was Lauren's stalker. Then Lauren could try her hardest to forget some crazy woman had made her life a nightmare for fourteen years. Her eyes flicked to Lauren and her heart warmed at the sight of her relaxed features. It then skipped a happy beat when Lauren told her mum she was moving back to London straight after the exhibition, and she couldn't wait for her to meet Emma.

A few minutes later, Lauren hung up and patted

the space beside her.

'I take it your mum was pleased to hear the news.'

'Ecstatic. I haven't heard her so happy in a long time. She can't wait to meet you either,' Lauren said and playfully poked her in the ribs.

Emma set her glass on the bedside table and sunk onto the bed. 'Do you blame her? Wouldn't you want to meet the woman who makes your daughter feel like she walks on air?' she said laughing.

'There is that.' Lauren pulled her down so they were lying side by side.

'So,' Emma said, closing the gap between them. 'Have you any idea how you want to go about approaching Mike's sister tomorrow?'

'That all depends on whether Mike keeps his promise and doesn't blab about me knowing.'

'And if he doesn't say anything?'

'Then I'll give her enough rope to hang herself with.'

'And then shop her to the police?'

'Do you think I should?'

'Do you need to ask? You're damn right you should let them know. What if she goes on to do this to someone else—if she hasn't already? Do you really want someone else to go through what you've been through?'

'No, you're right,' Lauren said.

'Why are you smiling?'

'Why do you think?'

It wasn't until she felt Lauren's warm breath against her naked chest that she realised Lauren had unbuttoned her shirt.

'You are so naughty.'

'Turn the light off and I'll show you how naughty I can be.'

Emma didn't need telling twice.

Chapter Thirty-Seven

Claire watched Lauren and Emma with surprise as they entered her shop, a fight or flight look crossing her features; apparently, Mike had kept his promise.

'I want no more trouble from you two. You—'

'The game's up, Claire.'

Claire shot her a querulous look. 'Game? What game?'

'The sick one you've been playing with me.'

'I don't—'

'You don't know what I'm talking about?' Lauren walked over to a bucket of flowers and snatched up the label card. 'You know what I have in my hand here?'

'Don't patronise me. It's a card—'

'—with your handwriting on it, which the police will compare to the handwriting that's on the letters you sent me.'

'That's how I know you're lying. Mike has—' She stopped abruptly and covered her mouth with her hand.

'Mike has what? The copies I gave him? I'm not stupid. I kept copies,' she bluffed. In her peripheral vision, she saw Emma frowning. 'And my parents have every vile piece of correspondence you sent me.'

That's good. Panic was showing in her eyes. Her only salvation was to tell the truth—or so Lauren thought. Almost as quickly as Claire's fear appeared, it dissipated.

'Oh please. You think I'm falling for that crap? If

you had all this evidence, you would have gone straight to the police and not come here looking for a confession. Get out of my shop. If I see either of you here again, I'll call the police myself.' She smirked and tossed her hair over her shoulder.

Emma gazed at her soberly. 'Oh dear. I'll give you that, Claire. You're a fighter.'

'Yes, and I always win.'

'Not this time you don't.' Emma withdrew her phone from her pocket and tapped it. Laying it on the counter in front of Claire, she stood back and crossed her arms as Mike's voice filled the air.

'Claire is the one who's been stalking you …'

'That fucking little shit,' she said, reaching for the phone.

Emma snatched it back. 'So you see, Claire, we don't need your confession to go to the police. We came by to ask for your side of the story before deciding what to do.'

Lauren thought Claire might shut down again, but to her surprise, Claire's face turned into a scowl and she moved around the counter to stand in front of her.

'Okay, Ms Lauren Wonderful. I followed you and took pictures of you because I wanted you to go away.'

'But why? What did I do to make you hate me so much?'

'What did you do? That's the point. You didn't have to do anything. You had everything laid at your feet while people like me barely got noticed. Well I showed you, didn't I?'

'Yes, Claire, you showed me all right,' Lauren said sadly. 'You showed me the lengths a bitter, twisted person will go to, and for what? Did your life improve after I left? Did you get what you wanted? Or is your life mediocre because you have so much darkness and bitterness in you that nothing good ever happens to you?'

'All that matters is that I won.'

'You didn't win. You see, everything I hold dear I still have. My family, friends'—she nodded at Emma—'someone who loves me. Do you even know what that feels like?'

Claire's eyes glassed over.

'No, I didn't think you did, and you never will until you stop dragging people down. There's enough happiness in the world for everyone. You should try and remember that.' Lauren turned to go. 'I hope this is the last time I ever hear from you.'

'And what if it isn't?'

It was Lauren's turn to spring a surprise on her. 'You see this on my button?'

Claire glanced at it.

'Look closer. You see that?' She pointed to the tiny camera lens. 'I have your confession on camera.'

She pulled out the camera and replayed the last five minutes on her phone.

'Let me tell you what will happen. I'm taking this evidence to the police. They might do something about it or they might not. If they don't, that's fine with me. If I so much as get an inkling that you're bothering me again, this little video will go mainstream: YouTube, Facebook, Twitter—you name it, you'll be on it. And if you don't think that's bad enough, I will bury your business too.'

Claire's mouth opened and closed.

'Good. I see we're on the same page. Emma, are you ready? I have a show to prepare for.'

Emma held out her arm and Lauren looped hers through it.

'So long, stalker,' Emma muttered under her breath.

They waited until they were around the corner before they jumped up and down on the spot.

'That was brilliant,' Lauren said. 'I really thought she wouldn't budge.'

'I know. What a hard-nosed cow. After all that, she still had the cheek to ask what you'd do if she kept stalking you.'

'I almost feel sorry for her. The only way she can get any happiness out of life is by bringing others down.'

'That's her cross to bear, not yours. Now let's get this footage to the police and then you need to go to work. You've only got a few days left before the big opening.'

'Yes, master.'

'I'll show you who the master is tonight,' Emma said, wiggling her brows.

Chapter Thirty-Eight

For the past few days, they'd hardly left the bedroom, not that Lauren was complaining.

They had just stepped out of the shower, and Emma approached her from behind while she was applying her make-up for the exhibition. Emma placed her hands around Lauren's breasts and nuzzled her neck.

'Emma, you're insatiable. We haven't got time,' Lauren half-heartedly protested.

'We can have a quickie. Ten minutes, max,' Emma said, already pulling Lauren out of the bathroom and towards her bedroom.

'Ten minutes?' Lauren asked, relenting. She decided she'd just apply some lipstick and eyeliner rather than the full works as she'd intended.

'That all depends on you,' Emma said.

All thoughts of her show swiftly left her mind when Emma closed the bedroom door and pushed her down on the bed.

In the end, Lauren had to call the taxi and rearrange the pickup time. They were expected at the gallery at five o'clock, and by Lauren's calculations, if the driver was fast, they'd just about make it.

Underneath her black cape, Lauren wore a black, strapless Dior dress and high-heeled shoes. Carefully crossing her legs, she sat back against her seat as the taxi whizzed along Albert Embankment.

'You're such a bad influence on me,' Lauren said to Emma, who was sitting next to her, holding her hand in both of her own. Emma's red dress seductively hugged her figure, and Lauren couldn't take her eyes off her exposed cleavage.

'And you love it, don't you?'

'Yes,' Lauren admitted with a ragged breath, thinking of how Emma's lovemaking literally took her breath away.

The driver took a sharp left and picked up speed to beat the red light.

'Good,' Emma said, staring at her through half-hooded eyes.

'Stop looking at me like that,' Lauren said, wanting nothing more than to tell the driver to take them back to her apartment so they could pick up where they'd left off. 'At this rate, I won't be able to think straight.'

Emma threw her a petulant look. 'I should hope not.'

'You have no worries on that front.'

The taxi ground to a halt outside the gallery.

Excitement rose in her. Not only because Emma was by her side, but because a mixture of people from all walks of life were heading into the gallery. She'd never doubted Frankie's abilities to get people through the door to see her work, but she was in a bit of disbelief that the project she had worked so hard on would be seen by people besides a select few.

'You nervous?' Emma asked as they stepped into

the gallery, holding hands.

'A little.'

Emma gave her a challenging look and she laughed.

'Okay, a lot, but in a good way.'

The atmosphere was buzzing with excitement and several of the well-dressed guests sipping on flutes of champagne looked like the arty type who had money to burn. *Just the sort Frankie loves.*

Georgie headed towards her with a group of chattering women dressed smartly in Chanel suits.

'Here goes,' Lauren murmured. 'Let the show begin.'

Lauren moved from guest to guest, answering questions about her work. When people commented on Lauren's glow, she and Emma shared a secret smile that reminded them of their lovemaking.

Lauren should have been concentrating on the positive comments guest were saying about her work and making small talk, but all she could think about was Emma and how long it would be before they were alone again.

'You look breathtakingly stunning,' Emma said when they found themselves alone.

Lauren eyed Emma appreciatively over the rim of her glass as she took a mouthful of champagne. 'So do you. If I could make all of these people disappear, I would in a second, and I'd—'

'What would you do?' Emma asked, kissing Lauren's neck.

The feel of Emma's soft lips pressing against her

skin sent a tide of tingles down her spine. She whispered her intentions into Emma's ear and Emma's face coloured.

'Ooh you are so bad.' She drew back and met Lauren's gaze, her eyes glassy, suddenly serious. 'You've got so much to be proud of. Look at all these people in awe of your talent. It's amazing.'

Emma was right. The way things were turning out was unbelievable. She couldn't have imagined this would be the outcome when she had accepted Frankie's offer to exhibit her work in London. The reception and great turn out of influential people was beyond her wildest expectations.

Lauren stroked Emma's cheek with the back of her hand. 'And with you by my side, this moment is even more special.'

'I'm glad to hear it,' Emma said in jest. 'Now don't worry about me. Go and mingle with your many adorers. You need to network now that you've made your name in London.'

'Uh-huh,' Lauren said distractedly as she glanced at the entrance. The sky had turned dark and she was beginning to think that the olive branch she'd extended to Hope hadn't worked.

'I'll socialise in awhile. I'm just waiting for a special guest to arrive.'

'More special than me?' Emma said with mock disappointment.

'That all depends on who you ask,' a familiar voice said from beside them.

'Hope! What are you doing here? Sorry, I didn't mean to say—Oh, you know what I mean.' Emma pulled Hope into her arms and hugged her tightly.

Hope pulled back a little. 'Can't a woman support her sister and her talented partner? Who knew our school would produce a force to be reckoned with in the art world?'

Lauren gave Hope a grateful smile, and Hope returned it, squeezing Lauren's hand.

'I've been looking at your photos, and I am truly impressed. I hope you'll sign the three images I bought. I'll be rich in a few years when they shoot up in value.'

Lauren laughed. 'Of course.'

'I'm so glad you came. I want to apologise—' Emma said.

'I think we both said a lot of things we didn't mean, and I'm not too stubborn to admit when I'm in the wrong. It's obvious to anyone that Lauren loves you very much.'

'Thank you, Hope.'

'I'll always be here, Emma. You're my little sister. I'll watch out for you whether you like it or not. Sometimes I'll get it wrong, but that's the thing about love. It's all about forgiveness.'

Emma pulled Lauren in for a group hug.

Now I can fully relax and enjoy the night. When Hope hadn't returned her numerous telephone calls asking her to get in touch with Emma, Lauren thought her pleas had fallen on deaf ears. She was happy to see they hadn't.

'Evening, ladies,' Frankie said as the women parted. 'Enjoying the show?'

'Loving it,' Emma said. 'You've done a great job.'

'All for a very special lady,' Frankie said, looking at Lauren. 'Good to see you here, Emma. I'm sure I'll be seeing you a lot more now that Lauren is coming back to London. Maybe we can start from scratch?'

'Definitely.' She reached down and took Lauren's hand.

'And you are?' He looked at Hope with interest.

Hope held out her hand. 'Emma's sister.'

Frankie's eyebrows rose. 'I hope I'll be seeing you as well.'

He smiled and excused himself.

'That man is hot! Why didn't you guys tell me about him?'

'He seems to like you,' Lauren said. 'Go and shower him with your charms while I borrow Emma for a moment. I have a surprise for her.'

'In that case I think I'll go and find Frankie.' Hope stood on her tiptoes and scanned the room. 'He's over there. I'll see you two later, or not, as the case may be.'

The women laughed as they watched her weave her way through the crowd.

'Come with me?' Lauren grabbed Emma's hand and led her to a section of the room she had banned her from venturing into.

'Close your eyes.'

Emma's eyes fluttered shut, and Lauren guided her around several people. She stopped and turned Emma to face a wall. Standing behind her, she slipped her arms around her waist.

'Okay, you can open them,' she whispered into her ear.

Hanging on the wall in front of them was Lauren's 'Alpha and Omega' series, only now there were two new additions. The first was a photograph of them taken in Emma's apartment, both on the sofa, entwined in each other's arms as they watched TV together. The second was an empty frame.

'When on earth did you take this?' Emma asked, turning around in Lauren's arms, her lips brushing against her mouth.

'I hope you don't mind. I set my camera to take pictures randomly, I wanted to catch us together naturally.'

'No of course not, it's absolutely beautiful. I just can't believe you put a photograph of us in your collection,' she said, a bemused look on her face. 'But what's with the empty frame? You planning on putting someone else there?'

Lauren rested her forehead against Emma's and gazed intently into her eyes. The love she felt for her shone back at her like a beacon. 'That, my darling, will be where the picture of our Omega goes.'

It would be fifty years later, after a lifetime of love and laughter, that Lauren's liver-spotted hand would slip the last photograph taken of her and Emma—both grey-haired and frail—into the empty frame. Their special connection would still be intact, the camera capturing their love that would last for an eternity, even after Mother Earth called them home.

Printed in Great Britain
by Amazon